A collection of stories centered around Christmas cookies.

Caramelized Pecan Cookie Holiday Hideaway by J.W. Garrett

Spritz Cookie Showdown by Melanie Hoffer

Candy Cane Cookie Cover-Up by Jael Allen

Gingerbread Men and Toad's Wart by Daniel Kamin

Dip in Chocolate

by

J.W. Garrett
Melanie Hoffer
Jael Allen
Daniel Kamin

Dip in Chocolate

Cover Art by *The Wild Rose Press, Inc.*

The Wild Rose Press, Inc.
PO Box 708
Adams Basin, NY 14410-0708
Visit us at www.thewildrosepress.com

Publishing History
First Edition, 2022
Trade Paperback ISBN 978-1-5092-4511-6

Published in the United States of America

Caramelized Pecan Cookie Holiday Hideaway

by

J.W. Garrett

Christmas Cookies

Dedication

To my grandparents who taught me everyone has a
story to tell.

"Sunny? I'm sorry. Really…"

Her boss's face didn't look sorry. In fact, Laura's mouth slid upward in a perfect imitation of the Cheshire Cat in *Alice in Wonderland*.

Suits her… Maybe I could freeze it like that for a couple hours. Just one tiny flick of the wrist and done. Sunny Yates dropped into her desk chair and swiveled away from her computer monitor. *Damn it! Four weeks until Christmas…* "I've never been fired," she announced quietly, more to herself than the woman in front of her.

"Not fired. Laid off," Laura corrected, laying a sagging cardboard box on Sunny's desk.

"Semantics."

"Once this interim team gets rolling, we'll see. I'm hopeful we can bring you back by June, July at the latest. How's that sound?"

Condescending, that's the word. Yeah… Sunny needed to eat, to pay rent in between now and then. Small little issues in the real world that needed to be dealt with. The woman's perky voice grated on Sunny's nerves. She rubbed at the throbbing pain mounting above her eyes.

She didn't need to hear the words again. They had cut enough the first time around. While shuffling through papers on her desk, she muttered a quick spell. Immediately Laura started sneezing—the loud and wheezing variety—one right after the other. Now who was smiling?

"I'll…*achoo, achoo*… Oh my…*achoo*." She raced from the room.

Sometimes being a witch came in handy.

Sunny's gaze scanned the Manhattan skyline. Drawn to the view, she rose and strolled the few steps necessary to take in the magnificence of the city from high above the melee and crowded streets below. This, she would miss. When she'd landed the position here at *One Perfect Life*, the magazine of her dreams, in her mind, she had made it. Had crossed over that invisible boundary to success.

Since Sunny graduated at NYU, she'd always had a plan to go it alone, to start her own business eventually. Steadily she'd been working to get there. Was this the right moment, though? Her hand might be forced either way, but she could try scrying tonight and maybe get a murky glimpse of what waited for her. Things weren't ever what they seemed when one peered into the future, though. So many variables were constantly shifting, and one's worldly prospects ever changing from one minute to the next. Her grandmother had taught her at a very young age to be careful, fully mindful, with such strong, volatile magic.

Outside, the icy chill of the day smacked her in the face, and with her hands full of the remnants from her last four years parceled down to one lonely box, she stepped onto the sidewalk. *Unemployed at Christmastime. Fa-la-la-la-la, la-la-la-la…* The day had turned miserable, like her mood had taken over the weather—which could actually happen if she weren't careful.

Decorations lined the streets, filled every store window, dangled from the traffic lights, and clung to car bumpers. Soon this devastating holiday would be over, and she could breathe a sigh of relief.

After the short drive home, Sunny fought the box up two flights of stairs, let herself into her apartment, and shoved the door closed, her thoughts alive with her new venture. Unceremoniously emptying her arms, she headed for her computer and logged in. She clicked on the folder where she'd stored all the data and her research during the past couple years related to her digital magazine start-up, *Endeavor*. Come January, she was launching this thing, her concept of a digital magazine devoted to those who wanted to pursue a lifestyle focused on holistic living.

First things first…

Before she could chicken out and change her mind, she called her landlord and notified him of her intention to vacate her apartment by next week. She was doing this. Living the dream. Putting her best foot forward. Striking out on her own… Also, she couldn't afford this place now anyway.

Sunny had needed this push. She could see that now. Maybe she could put a different spin on this, kinda like earning her wings so she could fly. More platitudes…

Besides, she couldn't fly per se, but she could apparate and levitate. Which led to her next issue—visiting the property she owned in upstate New York, in a tiny town called Willingham Creek. Her grandmother, Charlotte Dawson, who had died at the ripe old age of ninety-one, had bequeathed it to her. After Sunny's mom had left with no word, no letter, no explanation, Grandmother had taken Sunny in, had raised her like a daughter. God, she missed her.

Summoning the words needed from the family

grimoire, Sunny tossed her consciousness to the aging farmhouse. Maybe it wouldn't be as bad as she anticipated. Blinking her eyes open, she greeted a picturesque world, swirling in white.

****

Noah Russell dragged his gaze to the map on his SUV dashboard before peering out his window, searching the clouds currently spitting snow. The forecast called for more snowfall. Ten more minutes, per the GPS. His arrival should be before the worst of it.

His kids, Janie and Rob, eight and six, would love it here in Willingham Creek now, especially with the expectation of more of the white stuff right on through Christmas. Too bad his ex-wife, Elaine, didn't agree. Although their divorce had been relatively amicable, when it came to the holidays, the woman hadn't given an inch. Of course he could take her to court and win, gaining half their children's vacation time from their respective schools, but what would that get him for the long haul? He needed their relationship to stay on an even keel so if and when push came to shove, he'd have enough goodwill built up for the important stuff.

His mind turned to his latest business venture, *One Perfect Life*. Too many loose ends for his comfort to see this one tied up by the end of the month. His personal assistant, Alex, kept him up-to-date several times a day. Alex's team couldn't be beat for its ability, expertise, and efficiency. Noah wanted the deal closed by the thirty-first for many reasons. The magazine might be the last acquisition that he'd lead, for a while anyway. Other ambitions tugged at his heart. At thirty-nine he had more money than he could spend in a lifetime, even considering his ex-wife's cut.

What better timing could there be? His conglomerate, Russell Enterprises, was running at peak performance. A competent, experienced management team ran the daily operations with Noah's insight, guidance, and leadership. During this break he'd planned to mull over his future and make some decisions. So much more awaited him, but before fully committing to a new direction, he needed more time to mentally sort out all the adjustments this move would bring, along with the accompanying ripple effects within his enterprise.

Despite the cold, he slid down the car window and breathed in the fresh air. A wave of melancholy gripped his chest, as it always did when he first came to town. Family excursions, summer vacations, getaways… This place held so many childhood memories.

His tires crunched through the ice and snow, struggling to hang on to the road beneath him. The late-afternoon sun peeked through the cloud cover, teasing him with the temperature—only eighteen degrees out there, per his dashboard readout. Still plenty of time for his traditional first stop. Tension eased from his shoulders as he parked near the bookstore and grinned, the city's hold on him slowly loosening now in favor of Books and Treasures. Time seemed to evaporate once he passed through those doors.

Shoving his hands into gloves, Noah strolled to the bookstore from where he'd parked a block down the street, admiring the glowing lights shimmering from the establishments, their storefronts decked out in red and green, elves and Santas on full display. He waved and smiled at Cora, the store owner.

"Why, Noah, good to see you again. I was wondering if you'd make it here this year. Then I heard about the benefit."

"Yes, ma'am. I wouldn't miss it. Nothing like Willingham Creek during the holidays."

"Coffee on the house. Once you've decided on a book, that is."

He had already begun to peruse the best sellers from their perch in the display case. "Books," he corrected. "I plan to hunker down for a while. And thank you for the offer."

An hour later, four books resting on the table, he was several chapters into the latest novel from Stephen King. Nestled in by the stone fireplace, he sipped a latte, shedding more layers of the city with each page turned.

The Christmas bells hung from the front door jangled a merry greeting, and Noah lifted his nose from his book, checking out the new arrival. His gaze tracked the woman as she moved, unwrapping the scarf from her neck, freeing her chestnut brown hair to bounce over her shoulders. She unbuttoned her coat, showing off long, lean legs hugged tight by her jeans, which were tucked into snow boots.

Smart woman. Prepared. Not tromping in here from the city in ridiculous high heels and brand-name knockoffs, working at playing in the country. But she definitely wasn't indigenous to this small town either.

A red sweater clung to her middle, peeking out from behind her coat. Noah met beautiful women every day. Glamorous and even sexy behind their fake facades. But this woman was genuine, mesmerizing, strikingly so, and she made it appear effortless. She glanced up from her conversation with Cora, and his gaze locked with the newcomer's, trapped by the multitude of emotions flickering across her face. Something about her was different but in a good way. She blinked and flashed him a shy smile, instantly sending warmth through him. Who was she?

****

Heat throbbed through Sunny from the inside out. What the hell was that? Felt like leftover energy from a spell of some sort. But she hadn't conjured one in several hours. She shrugged out of her coat, refocusing on the woman in front of her giving recommendations for takeout places. The fast-food chains she frequented in the city weren't here, due to their special regulations apparently. Restaurants had to work hard to serve the people of this place. Took time…money… Maybe this tiny town wasn't worth the effort for the franchises. Everything was a mom-and-pop-type business here. Maybe the food would be healthier too?

Sunny lost herself in the series of instructions and hand motions thrown in for good measure, as Cora gave detailed directions to Harry's Hamburgers just down the street.

"Thanks, but I don't eat red meat," she explained when she caught the man's gaze again, intent on her from across the room.

Cora continued on her rant, but Sunny tuned her out as she straightened, pivoted toward the stranger, who looked as if his face could be chiseled from stone, given the beautiful symmetry of angles there.

"Ah…strikes your fancy, does he? If only I were a little younger. But, truth be told, I'm old enough to be his…mother. So…"

"Excuse me? Mother?" *Grandmother for sure.* Sunny gave her a discreet up-and-down look.

"Oh, I know, dear. Give an old woman her

daydreams."

The man's well-dressed and slim physique kept Sunny's eyes riveted, his lips curving up slightly as their gazes touched again. His wind-blown sandy brown hair made her want to run her fingers through it.

"That's Noah Russell. Quite the businessman. Born in this very town before going off to the city and earning his millions. That's a fact."

"Millions?" Sunny coughed. "Wow…" *Outta my league for sure*. She watched as a young man approached Mr. Russell, newspaper in hand. A stoic facade washed over Noah's face as he stood, shook hands with the stranger, then autographed the paper.

"He made the local and national news again. So many times now I've lost track."

Sunny made a mental note to check her mail. Read up on the man. Her postal service had just begun three days ago, and she'd signed up for the local paper. With any luck she'd get a copy.

"Thank you for the information." Sunny grabbed her book purchase. "I can't wait to sample some coffee and read in that nook over there"—she gestured—"sometime soon. My boxes await, and they won't unpack themselves."

"Please do come again."

"Oh, I will. I love the ambiance of this place. Warm. Cozy. Inviting."

"Thanks for stopping by."

Sunny stepped to the doorway, adjusting her things in her arms, then putting them all in the nearby chair. She had been here long enough to shed her coat and scarf and gloves. Now she had to don them all again before stepping outside. Head down, adjusting her gloves and gripping her bag with her purchase, she took a step. In the span of a few seconds, the bells danced above her head, the door held ajar by a masculine hand. And she leaned into a door that suddenly wasn't there. Then she was flying. And not in the levitating manner she was used to.

Strong arms grabbed her and settled her on her feet, a dark stream of coffee dripping a slow path down her coat.

"Sorry. I'm so sorry." Noah held her steady as he examined the spill his coffee had made when their bodies collided exiting the store. "I'm not normally this clumsy." His green eyes flashed concern while he dug his hand in his pocket and fished out a napkin. "Kids," he offered with a crooked smile. "Seems I'm always cleaning up something."

"It's fine. Really it is. I'll throw it in the washer. Do you always bowl girls over this way?"

"Actually, no." He chuckled. "I'd bought the coffee for you. It was to be an icebreaker. When I saw you leaving, I rushed to get it to you, forgot a lid, and, well, you know the rest. Bottom line…I've made quite a mess of things."

"You're Mr. Russell?"

"Noah, please." He shook her hand. "I see Cora gave you an introduction on my behalf."

Sunny swallowed her laughter, heat rising in her cheeks. How did he do that to her? "You've certainly got a fan in that character."

"Eh…" He tilted his head. "More like a family member. Cora's known me since I was a kid. And you are?"

"Oh, Sunny. My name's Sunny."

"Sunny." Laughter danced in his vivid green eyes as her name rolled off his tongue. "Meet me tomorrow for coffee. Let me make it up to you. We can come back here to the scene of the crime, and I'll try to prove to you that I'm not a bumbling idiot."

Kids… He'd mentioned his kids. Was a wife in the picture also? No ring…*hmm…* "Truthfully I'm just moving in. I could use a few days to settle in. I'm a bit out of sorts myself, with boxes everywhere and a new business I'm handling remotely."

"How about the end of the week, then?"

"Uh, sure."

"Could I have your phone for just a minute?"

"Okay." She slid her phone into his hand.

Within thirty seconds he'd added his contact information and a coffee date to her calendar, Saturday, five days from now. "How's that?" he asked, his gaze finding hers again for affirmation.

"Sounds good."

He grasped her hand that she hadn't managed to glove up yet and kissed it lightly. "Nice to meet you." He canted his head. "Until next week when I'll make a better impression. I promise." He crouched down and gathered his wayward books, then wrapped his scarf twice around this neck.

Mmm. She sniffed the air. Some manly soap accented with a scent of pine. Made her want to follow him. Instead she watched him stroll leisurely down the sidewalk, stopping every few yards to offer a greeting to those he met. *Maybe not the typical rich guy.*

Waving a hand over the front of her coat, Sunny relegated the stain to nothing more than a pleasant memory of their unusual *crash and meet*. But the man exuded a powerful aura, radiating outward from him in ripples of red. No doubt its radiance drew her to him.

Glancing down at his newly entered contact, she grinned. Beside the name *Noah*, he'd added two emojis. One an explosion, the other a coffee. Yep. Pretty much summed it up.

Soon her front door squeaked, announcing her return. Tossing her keys on the kitchen counter, she sighed, then shuffled her way around the boxes to the stairs. From a step she retrieved the family grimoire and headed to Grandmother's bedroom upstairs and the cedar chest that held so many memories hidden within its trunk.

During the long drive from the city, her grandmother's spirit had accompanied Sunny, guiding, leading, cheering her on to her new destination. The drive had given Sunny time to think as she embarked on a new job, in a small town—the very same town Sunny's mom had left, never to return. Sunny never knew her father. Not so much a sad memory, just a fact. Back then—at Christmastime too—she had been only eight. None of it made any sense.

But moving in with her grandmother did. The two made the move to Queens. Best for Sunny's future education, per Grandmother. Patiently, day by day, Sunny learned the power of her magic, the wisdom found in the family grimoire, all at her grandmother's knee.

"Someday you will be a powerful witch," she repeated to Sunny on a daily basis. "Feel the energy emanate from the grimoire and practice your lessons. You'll see."

Every day after school, her real learning would begin. Opening the weathered tome, she'd pause, waiting for the pages to settle on the lesson for the evening. By the night's end, when the flutters of paper quieted and her mind rested, Sunny was grateful for the knowledge she gained.

Growing up in Queens had kept Sunny honest. Kept her tough. But her grandmother had given her strength and balance. Imbued her with her presence that still remained with Sunny, even after Grandmother had died six months ago.

Since Sunny's graduation from NYU five years ago, Grandmother had been here, in Willingham Creek. But Sunny had never come to visit, too busy with her New York City life—her career—to make the time. They'd visited through their magical bond often, though. Now, with Sunny wrapped in a musty blanket, seated among her grandmother's most treasured items, the toll of the years away from her became unbearable. The time lost unforgiveable. Only now the full weight hit her shoulders.

Not lost, child, just delayed, she heard in her head. *Prepare yourself. You're home.*

****

The bright sun streamed through the window, the shards of light warming her face in the chill of the early morning. Sunny scooted deeper into the covers, nestled between several quilts. Blinking her eyes open and stretching, she met resistance. All around her, the contents of her grandmother's cedar chest littered the floor of the upstairs master bedroom. Regretting her decision to not move to the bed before falling asleep last night, she slid from the covers to the stone fireplace.

Summoning the element of fire, drawing on its power, she struck the logs gathered there with a ball of flame writhing at her fingertips. Within minutes, warmth licked away the cold air, reaching outward, disseminating from the tongues of fire gently crackling in the fireplace.

Better, much better. After collecting the items that needed addressing into a small heap, she slid on slippers and threw on another sweater before attending to more pressing needs…a bathroom stop and coffee.

The floorboards groaned in protest under her feet as she sped down the hallway. This place needed renovations, among them an en suite bathroom for the master bedroom, pronto. The electrical wiring needed to be redone, the kitchen remodeled, and the roof replaced, just for starters. But another full bathroom? That took priority. At least the one existing bathroom had been remodeled when her grandmother moved back in here. All the rest would have to wait, though, until Sunny got her digital magazine, *Endeavor*, up and running. Today she'd spend some time on that too.

A smile took her lips. She found herself oddly invigorated with the new day. Things were looking up from her mortifying exit of the city to the tune of *Merry Christmas* and *Happy Holidays* as she'd left her coworkers. Maybe she'd made the right decision for a leap of faith right now.

At least she wasn't totally caught off guard. This business was brutal. And with yet another reorganization of the magazine, *One Perfect Life*, she had seen the writing on the wall months ago. After the new year would have been better timing to leave, though. She would have had more money saved, due to the Christmas bonus she'd been promised. Of course, that's most likely one of the reasons she'd been laid off now.

She shrugged, allowing the positivity more leeway. Time would tell.

The coffee gurgled happily beside her as Sunny leaned against a kitchen barstool, opened her note app, and updated her to-do list for *Endeavor* that she'd address today. The coffee's aroma drifted through her senses. She let loose a tiny moan. What would she do without this dark, delicious concoction? After devouring a piece of toast, she trotted back upstairs to her bedroom, set her coffee on the nightstand, and plopped down on the floor to pick up where she'd left off last night.

Her hand glided over the worn leather cover of her grandmother's journal. Over the years Sunny had witnessed her grandmother writing in its pages, most often during early morning hours, before she started her long days. While in Queens the tenacious woman had worked early mornings at a local dry-cleaning shop and afternoons at a diner—where she had whipped up the most delicious desserts. Sunny personally tasted most of them daily when she stopped by for a snack and an hour of homework after school. Then, when Grandmother had finished her shift, the two would walk home together, a precious time for Sunny to share the details of her day with the one person who truly cared.

She flipped through the aged journal, carefully turning the pages as she read, reliving moments she remembered, but mostly discovering Grandmother's struggles that she'd kept deeply hidden. The joy in her life had stemmed from Sunny—it was clear by her reading—but also passing on what knowledge of the craft that Grandmother could. That bond held them together across time and space.

This time of year had been difficult for them. But

Grandmother had made the holidays magical, with her enchanted decorations and spells that animated the small number of presents. Mostly, though, Sunny remembered Grandmother's Christmas cookies. Around mid-December, when they set to work on the caramelized pecan cookies, Sunny had felt a warmth in her heart that lasted the entire season, well after the delectable treats were gone. And in front of her, on the page, was Grandmother's original hand-penned recipe. How long had it been since Sunny made them? She couldn't even hazard a guess.

The paper fluttered back and forth between her fingers, returning her focus to the old recipe. "Okay, Grandmother," she whispered. "I'll make them if you promise to be with me in spirit." The journal slipped from her hands, the pages standing at attention, then easing open once again in a leisurely, slow dance. A hot tear slid down her cheek, followed by another. She wouldn't be alone this Christmas, not with her grandmother's spirit so alive and present in this old, rundown place.

Next week, I promise, Grandmother. Moving on to the next item, she lifted the jewelry box lid on a necklace she'd received from her grandmother on Sunny's sixteenth birthday. The gem, a cat's-eye opal, took her breath away, just as it had when she received it. So overwhelmed with its significance, she had given it back to her grandmother for safekeeping.

When witches of her line came of age at sixteen, the traditional gift from parents was this beautiful stone. The lore stated that the stone would find its mated gem, and, during that process, the witch who'd come of age would find her life partner too. A smile lifted her lips. No time line existed for this magic to come to fruition, however, and many witches in her family had died as spinsters. Given that fact, Sunny didn't attribute much weight to the prophesy out in the real world today.

Rolling the stone around in her hand, she examined the sparkling blue and green tones. The time had come for the beautiful gift to see the light of day. Not that she believed she'd find a mate anytime soon but more because the magic inherent in the piece would be enhanced when worn by its intended recipient. Who knew what could develop if given a chance? Enchanted items typically worked in unexpected ways.

Warmth pulsed from the gift, seeping into her skin. She let its effects course through her, then laid it on her nightstand, glancing at the time on her phone. Tonight she'd have time to read more from her grandmother's journal. The rest of the items she'd sift through later. They too deserved her full attention.

Work. Sunny's baby, *Endeavor*, called to her.

After arranging everything she needed at the kitchen table, she poured herself another cup of hot, black goodness and pulled up her spreadsheet, populated with her latest audience projections.

Through her research she'd found that her target market included those interested in the health of mind and body, organic farming, reducing their carbon footprint, combating the impacts of climate change, and achieving and maintaining the right balance in one's life. The topics were practically endless. Using her own stats, gathered from her premarketing efforts, she'd already begun an email listing, had her logo and branded graphics to match.

Her first monthly issue would cover an introduction

into the future topics already lined up for the first twelve months, thanks to her crowd-sourcing campaign, which detailed where readers' interests lay. Sign-ups for the new online-only venue were ongoing. But since Sunny had a full-time "safe" job, her business venture would never get the nurturing it needed. Now it would.

Nodding as she reviewed the data, she focused on her largest target groups. Here was where she would funnel her resources, creating ads to reach that twenty-five to thirty-five age group, followed closely by the fifty-plus tribe.

She would tailor an ad for those in between also. Their needs were different, more family oriented, though, thus more tweaking needed. Sunny would woo them in too. This way of thinking was a lifestyle choice.

Her phone vibrated. The contact popped up as Noah.

—Remember me. The coffee klutz? Need anything? This place can be quite an adjustment for those who aren't used to the small-town atmosphere.—

Wow… He must have gotten my phone number when he entered his in my contacts.

—Hey there. Oddly enough I'm adapting nicely. Strange how I don't miss the hustle and bustle of the big city. Maybe that'll come later. Gotta lot to take care of right now.—

—Reach out if I can lend a hand. Happy to help. See you "downtown" (laughing emoji) in a few days.—

—I'll be there.—

—(heart emoji)—

What? Her own heart skipped a beat. She stared at the screen until it flickered to black. She couldn't wait to see the charming Noah again either. She shouldn't respond…should she? *Keep him guessing.* That was the only card she could play for now. She squealed. *Okay...pull it together. It's just coffee. Back on task. Back to work. But Noah… Ohhhh...that mighty fine and sexy business mogul.*

Damn… Until Saturday…

She paused before her laptop, then typed in his name. She'd meant to take care of this earlier. With everything going on, it had taken a back seat. Her query returned immediately with over ten-million hits. The man had his own Wikipedia page… *My goodness.*

She scrolled down, her gaze skimming past mostly business-related articles, followed by social media contacts, Russell Enterprises details, all on the first page. Pictures lined the bottom of her screen—his family and what looked like dates he'd had, appearances, all with different women standing by his side in each shot. Her mouse hovered over page two. She cleared the search. This wasn't the way she wanted to get to know the man, based on the media's perspective of him. From their initial meeting she'd sensed the many layers inherent in Noah. Taking the time to let them unfurl, as they discovered each other, would be worth the wait. She was sure of it.

****

Noah eased back in his home-office chair, just finishing up a call with his kids; they'd been bubbling with enthusiasm, busy with their Saturday activities. He purposefully segmented his life into two broad categories—business and his kids. Made things simple, clear cut. One bucket or the other. He liked it that way. The relationships he'd entered into with women since his divorce had been more business related, really. Necessary for events he attended in most cases. No strings attached because he didn't want to go the opposite route.

His cursor blinked at him, still on the email he'd been typing when the kids' call had come through. With where his mind was headed, his focus was shot, though.

A sliver of doubt worked through his thoughts, making him question the efficiency of his system that provided boundaries and structure to his life. The anticipation of seeing Sunny again sparked feelings in Noah he'd believed were long dead. After his ex-wife had shredded his heart, he'd tucked that part of him safely away. That meant he wouldn't need to *feel* anything, in the love department anyway. Relationships without that specific component ruled his life now.

Only his kids survived that culling of himself.

After his children were born, he'd envisioned his kids spending carefree days here—boating, fishing, skiing, or just daydreaming—and he vowed at that time to give them the gift they could always return to, one that would always be there for them—a childhood that included Willingham Creek.

In bits and pieces it would come together for his two, but Thanksgiving wasn't quite the same experience with the kids as Christmas would have been. A long weekend wasn't enough to immerse them fully in the town he loved and his ex-wife hated. Soon, though, Janie and Rob would be on the bandwagon. The last time they'd visited, they'd been six and four. Too long ago. They were the perfect age to rediscover the town and join in the less-commercialized adventures of this place. Out of the city. Away from the filth and the crowds. Leaving behind the twenty-four-seven mentality that his ex-wife reveled in and that he fought to tamp down. But he'd see to it. He'd endure. And in the end, he'd win. Because it's what he did each and every day.

He returned to his email, intent on clearing out his inbox. He forwarded one to Alex for a priority response, categorized others into folders, and set reminders on the time sensitive communication that he wanted to answer personally. Then he closed the laptop, letting his churning thoughts take him.

Family ties bound everything together for Noah. When his brother, James, had died, returning "home" had been too much for a while. That bond had never weakened, and his brother became one of the deciding factors driving the shift in Noah's business decisions moving forward. James had lost his battle with leukemia at eighteen. With only two years difference in their ages, the pair had been inseparable. Back then, working with others, fighting the battle of this insidious disease, like his brother had, had given Noah's grief a needed outlet. Now, well, it called to him again. But the pull was stronger, causing him to question his personal and business priorities now.

Almost a decade ago, with the help of many collaborating business partners and individual donations, Russell Enterprises had founded the James Russell Foundation. At thirty, when Noah had finally gotten it off the ground and hired a team to manage the day-to-day operations, he'd thought it would remain small compared to the rest of his business entities. But now, just nine years later, that arm of Russell Enterprises had found a global reach, and he felt a draw to return to this specific business of his that held a piece of his heart cradled within it.

And in a few weeks, he'd personally attend the

charity event that Willingham Creek held every year on behalf of the James Russell Foundation. With the notable exception of being in the company of his kids, there wasn't any place Noah would rather be. If all went according to plan, he would have an announcement during the event. He was almost one hundred percent certain but needed this short respite to reflect on what the change would mean for him in the months and years ahead.

Already in their early sixties, Noah's parents, Jessie and Tom, had migrated south to Florida years ago. Still, they returned on occasion; he was hoping they could make the trip for the upcoming benefit, but they hadn't committed just yet.

Noah sucked in a breath, letting it invigorate him. Time passed differently here, the air not quite so heavy, instead ripe with the changes that had quickened within him, almost like an affirmation of his choices.

His phone lit—Alex. *Damn. Already cutting it close.*

Noah had trained her to be respectful of his time. Had to be important. He picked up the call. Immediately she delved into multiple issues.

Noah's phone alarm buzzed, interrupting Alex's litany of updates, most of those surrounding his most recent acquisition, *One Perfect Life*. He hated that name. It had an undercurrent of the unattainable. *No one has a perfect life.* People would subconsciously shy away from the magazine, and that would be a hard battle to fight when it wasn't a variable that could be quantified. No doubt it was costing them readership. Market analysis, including A/B testing, would guide the transition team to a much better option. He was certain of it.

"Alex. We agree. Hand it off to the transition team.

I'm confident you'll lead them to a much better name for the magazine. Anything else pressing?" A beat of silence. "Good. I've got another appointment."

"*Hmm*. Not my business, but aren't you supposed to be vacationing, taking it easy before the benefit? And it's Saturday if you haven't noticed."

Of course he'd noticed, had been waiting for the day, the hour, that he'd see Sunny. He felt like a teenager again, unable to focus, while his thoughts continually returned to their chance meeting last week. The woman had devastated his concentration ever since. Maybe he was having an early midlife crisis. Maybe it was being back here in Willingham Creek at Christmastime. Maybe it was fate.

Noah was always on point, laser-focused, ready for anything life threw at him. He couldn't have attained the levels of success he'd reached without it. People called him The Terminator behind his back for good reason, for Christ's sake, and actually he didn't mind the nickname. "You know me, Alex. All business, no matter the day, no matter the hour."

"I do."

He could practically visualize the grin in her tone.

"More is behind this…*meeting* than just business, but I'll leave it at that. For now."

"Thank you, Alex. As always your perception is right on target."

"That's why they call me *Predator*."

"That's why I'm fortunate you're working for me."

"I won't let you forget it."

"Talk later."

"One more thing before you go. We do need to discuss your speech for the upcoming benefit."

"I've got some notes, points I want to focus on."

"Email them to me. I'll add mine and then send them to your speechwriter."

He navigated to the document on his phone. "Hitting Send now. Thanks."

Noah jabbed the button to end the call and strode down the hallway to his bedroom. His five-minute alert clocked down to four. He pocketed his phone and glanced in the mirror. Was this casual enough? The red cashmere sweater was warm, soft, and, above all, comfortable. And it didn't look too bad on him. All those nasty protein shakes and his personal trainer's rigorous workout sessions did make a difference. He shoved his feet into snow boots and circled the navy cashmere scarf around his neck. He took the steps two at a time, dashed through the kitchen and into the mudroom. Snatching his hooded coat and messenger bag from the hook by the door, he headed out. He'd planned to be early, wanted to watch her walk in. Wanted to see those gorgeous hazel eyes fill with wonder. He wanted…*ah hell…*

****

A chilly ten-minute ride later, Noah parked and sauntered into Books and Treasures. Even though the temperature had fallen to five below today, he felt invigorated by the brisk short walk from his parking spot. Nodding a hello to Cora, ordering croissants and lattes for two, he secured a place by the roaring fire, then settled into his chair, pulled out a newspaper from his messenger bag, and waited. He glanced to the door, checked his phone. Not time yet for another five minutes. No worries. He could feign interest in the news until then.

His phone vibrated.

—Just walking in.—

"Right on time…" Capturing this moment now made his early trek worth it.

Sunny's gaze searched for him. Noah could see her perfectly, a slight panic rising on her delicate features. As Noah stood and waved her over, her lips eased upward.

"Hello again. I wasn't sure you'd show."

"Really?" Her breath caught. "It's not every day a girl gets asked out to coffee in Willingham Creek by Noah Russell." She threw her coat over the back of a chair and sat down. "So cozy. Maybe I should spend some time writing in here during the week."

A café member brought over Noah's order. "Hope it's okay with you. I ordered us lattes and chocolate croissants. I promise. You'll love them."

Her eyes flashed surprise, then she grinned. "Oh my…these smell like heaven."

"So you're a writer in the city?"

"Yeah."

He tracked her tongue as it slid across her lips to catch some wayward chocolate filling, and struggled to focus on her next words.

"*Was* in the city."

He tuned back in.

"I was let go recently. My former company is in the process of a transition, an acquisition. I'm sure you've never heard of it—a magazine called *One Perfect Life*."

Her eyebrows arched up in question, then furrowed with worry as he sputtered and choked.

"Are you okay?"

Noah jogged his head, still coughing. The coffee and bite of pastry had gone down the wrong pipe.

She crouched by his side. "You better say something, or I'm going to Heimlich you."

That made him smile as he caught the scent of her perfume. Light. Sensual. Lovely… He dragged in another whiff of her and squeezed her hand. "I'm okay. Please, sit," he rasped out.

She eyed him warily, like he still might keel over, giving him a few more seconds to think. *Shit…* He needed to talk to Alex. How many employees had they let go right before Christmas? These trivial details didn't typically concern him. Only the bottom line. This outcome wasn't uncommon when restructuring debt, furloughing staff, renegotiating contracts—all of it already had his advance approval in order to assist the prospective company to achieve the buyout price agreed upon in the contract. "Please, continue."

Sunny sat a little straighter. "Well, I've decided to give it a go on my own. Not real sure why I'm telling a complete stranger this. I've been working on my plan for a while now, though, and I decided this was just the push I needed." Her eyes narrowed over the rim of her cup, locking with his. "If I fall on my face, maybe I can sue them, right?"

She could try. Sure. But she wouldn't be successful. He decided on another route. "Congratulations. Being your own boss is great. Let me know if I can help you in any way." This was when he should come clean. Right now. Throw everything on the table. But she'd bolt. He felt it in his bones. He could hear twinges of hurt in her voice, that pain she would then attribute to him if he told her. This way maybe he could offer some advice for her startup while getting to know what made this beautiful creature tick.

25

Noah maneuvered the conversation to her interests, then family and schools attended. Each catch of her breath, the twinkle in her eyes, her soft laughter, he memorized them all so he could relive them later. He hadn't fallen this hard, this fast, in so long. She stunned him, inside and out.

"Why the name Sunny if you don't mind my asking?"

"My given name is Susan. Once it was just me and my grandmother, *Sunny* just kinda evolved over time. Grandmother said she could see the sun in me every day. So why not make it official?"

The soft tinkle of her laughter jolted Noah to his core. "I agree," he mumbled.

"What did you say?"

"I said I'd like to meet her."

"Oh, well, she passed away."

"I'm sorry."

"I am too, for me. But she lived a wonderful life. I aspire to be like her."

"I'm sure you will be, from the fire I've seen inside you this afternoon. What was her name? Maybe I've met her."

"Charlotte Dawson. The last few years she didn't get out much. Not in the best of health. So she kept mostly to herself."

"Name sounds familiar. With college, then living in the city, I didn't make many trips back here for a while. Only for holidays. That's all changed now. But quite possibly my parents knew her. I'll check with them."

"She was quite a special lady. Speaking of which…she left me a big old house that I need to get back to. So much to be done. Hopefully it won't fall apart around me before I can fix it up." She straightened. "Maybe we can do this again sometime? I think I overshared and didn't leave you much time to speak up."

He rose to his feet, tracking her movement, captivated, as her face bent into a frown with the tiniest of pouts evident on her lips. He eased toward her, giving her plenty of time to back away if she chose to. But, sharing the same air space, she stood her ground. When his lips brushed hers, a slight gasp of breath left her. *Perfect*. She smiled against him, her mouth softening underneath his.

"I'd really like that," he whispered. "How about now?"

"What?" she asked, setting off a round of giggles. Her cheeks flushed a pretty pink.

"Invite me to see your house. I won't stay long. You've got a lot going on with the move, but I can put you in touch with some good contractors after I see what your needs are."

"Sure. That'd be great. But I wasn't kidding when I said the place was a mess. Don't judge me, please."

Noah's hand fell to her waist. "Lead the way. We should get you home, though. I didn't realize the time," he added, with a glance at his phone. "And a winter storm warning. Looks like it could be a bad one coming."

****

"Your research is sound. I'm impressed. And I like the route you're taking with your digital magazine. The market is there. The customer base. I say go for it, and good riddance to the rest."

Sunny scrutinized Noah, taking in his quick assessment of her work that had taken years to accumulate.

After a quick tour, he had compiled a short list of local businesses for her to contact to address her specific needs. He nodded his approval, his eyes still scanning the room. "The house has character. I like it."

"Which parts specifically? The holes in the ceiling, the drafty rooms, the ancient wiring, the old pipes?"

"The original hardwood floors, the spacious feel, the magnificent stone fireplace that extends to the second-floor bedroom, the wainscoting, the crown molding, and that's just the beginning of what I see."

"You do sound like you've done this before."

He huffed out a breath. "Renovating? You bet. Wait until you've seen my place."

"I'd like that."

He pulled her into the V of his legs and kissed her. Patiently he teased her mouth open, and his tongue slid inside, grazing hers. "*Mmm*," he groaned, tightening his fingers on her hips. "You taste so good."

"Wow, that was hot." She dragged her fingers along the strong line of his jaw. "Stay a little longer. If you want to, that is. I'm gonna make cookies this afternoon, my grandmother's famous caramelized pecan cookie recipe."

"I'd be honored to help. How about I build us a fire first?"

"Sure, I'll get the ingredients out we need to get started."

A few minutes later ribbons of flame sputtered and popped, its heat reaching out, warming the room with a tranquil glow. Sunny poured wine and sipped intermittently as she measured and sifted, combined and comingled. Soon the first batch went into the oven.

Noah chuckled. "Complicated recipe, but I'm rusty

at this. Baking's not really my forte."

"That's okay. I can tell you excel in other areas."

He grinned, his biceps straining against that perfect red sweater of his.

She let her mind drift for a few seconds to those washboard abs she was sure existed underneath those layers. "Tell me about your kids." They both eased onto the kitchen barstools.

Almost three bottles of wine and six batches of cookies later, he glanced out the window. "Come quick. You can just see the sun dipping under the horizon."

Despite the buzz in her head, she crossed the room in a hurry, taking the outstretched hand he offered. He pulled her into the circle of his arms, resting her body against his chest.

"Breathtaking," she murmured.

"Yes, you are," he added, his lips pressing kisses to the column of her neck.

"What do you think of the cookies?" She angled her head to give him more room to work, each touch of his mouth sparking a delicious sensation inside her.

He paused. "I was trying to gather the courage to ask if you'd consider making more for the fundraiser I'm hosting soon. They are melt-in-your-mouth fantastic. I'll bet you could sell these all around town."

"Let me make us some dinner while you tell me more about the event."

****

Noah cracked open his eyes. Last night had been a blur of Sunny's intoxicating scent, her grandmother's special cookies, and too much wine. One minute they'd been discussing the charity event, the next drinking. He rolled onto his back. How did the woman drink so much?

He'd barely kept up. She would put his buddies to shame. Suspiciously eyeing the quilt covering him, he peeked underneath the edges. *Okay. Good. Pants intact*. Tension eased from his muscles. If and when the time was right, they'd be together. He wanted to remember that experience, not have it flash by in a drunken stupor.

Sunny was special. Okay…there. He'd admitted it. He had practically given up on dating for now. Women wanted him for his money and prestige, and he was so sick of their games. Much easier to keep them categorized into his "business bucket." Until Sunny came along, his little piece of sunshine, and he wanted her to know it, wanted her to light each and every one of his days. Now and in the future. He only needed to get her on board now. *Jesus…* He had never been so completely taken by any one woman in his life. He shook his head at his luck.

The coffeepot perked to life nearby, bubbling out a rhythm before he smelled the aroma that pulled him out from the covers to the kitchen where he worshiped it, silently waiting with the empty mug he'd fished out of a box marked *Cups and Charms*. By the time the light *thud* of Sunny's feet announced her presence, he felt his humanity returning, already one cup in.

"Morning, Noah. How'd you sleep?"

"Morning, Sunshine. Like the dead. You?"

"Perfectly."

"Maybe we could consider sharing sleeping accommodations. Then maybe my status would lift to *perfectly* also."

His Sunshine spit out her coffee.

"Don't worry. I'm only partially kidding." He yanked her close. "Yesterday was the best day I've had in a very long time. Only to be outdone by today, I predict. I have a full schedule planned, now that I've gotten my body on board."

"Do these plans include me?"

"They do, indeed. I'll just go home, shower, and change. Won't take long."

She tossed a glance outside. "Snow's really coming down out there. You can shower here if you like."

"Snow doesn't bother me. But that would get us going on the agenda quicker."

"Up the stairs, take a right, first door on the left. I'll make breakfast."

He gulped down the last of his second cup of coffee, then scooped up his phone, shirt, and sweater. "I won't be long."

Jabbing the speed dial button for Alex, he took the steps two at a time.

"Noah, how can I help you this morning?"

"I only have a few minutes." He shut the bathroom door behind him. "Tell me what you know about the staffing reduction at *One Perfect Life*. You can call me back if you need to."

"No, we don't have those specific numbers. I can get them if you'd like. Who and how many is up to their current management team. We gave them a bottom-line number to meet. How they get there is their problem, as you've reminded our other acquisition targets in the past."

Right…all business, except this time. He winced. Come January, a management team from Russell Enterprises would be on-site. He could intervene and have her brought back on… *Hell…* The deal was done. Besides, Sunny had a damn good shot to make a go of it on her own. He could step in, offer a hand when she needed it. Bottom line, with the talent he'd glimpsed within her research and stats, his Sunshine was better off going it solo. "Think I'll stay outta the weeds. Thanks for the reminder."

"Sure. Anything else, boss?"

"Not now."

He turned on the shower faucet and stepped underneath the gloriously hot streams of water, rotating his body so they pounded his back. This room had definitely been renovated. Ten minutes later, clean but in the same clothes as yesterday, he strode back to the kitchen, feeling ten times better than he had earlier this morning. If needed, he always had the two changes of clothes in his car, one appropriate for business, the other more casual attire. These could last him another day. Besides, the ones he had on fit better for the festive activities he'd planned for them.

"What a fantastic shower," he announced as he entered the kitchen. "I feel like a new man."

Sunny smirked. "The old one was fine as is."

"Thank you, I think." *Wait for it… Here it comes…*

"How old are you? If you don't mind my asking." *There it is.* "Thirty-nine."

"Ah." She turned back, busy flipping pancakes.

"Was that a good ah or a bad ah?"

She turned to glance at him over her shoulder. "Age is relative. Just a number. I'm twenty-seven, by the way."

"Sounds perfect. And I agree."

She plated their breakfast. "Dig in. More coffee?"

"I'll get it. Sit." He poured refills for them. "Ready to hear the details regarding what's first today?"

Her answering smile brightened her face. Sunshine…pure and simple.

"Yes!" She bobbled in her seat, adding her own excited punctuation.

"I'll show you after we finish eating. You see, I took the liberty of picking up a few things yesterday. Hope you don't mind. We'll call them housewarming gifts."

"Sounds exciting. So while we eat, tell me about your wife. Janie and Rob are with her now, I guess. You won't see them for Christmas?"

"Ex-wife," he corrected. "Elaine will bring them up for the charity event at the end of the month. Willingham Creek isn't her favorite place, to put it mildly," he said around a bite. "She enjoys the Christmas glitz of the city. Me? I'd rather the kids get a more well-rounded perspective of the holidays. When they're a little older, I'll push for that. I had them for Thanksgiving." His sigh came out a growl. "And I'll have them for New Year's. That means about five days here before she gets them back."

"That must be hard." She slid her hand on top of his.

Rubbing her hand with his thumb, he met her gaze. "It is. But soon the kids will pick when they come and go. I want them to choose here. That's my plan—to expose them to the town where they can live wholesomely, learn to dream, fully enjoying what it can offer, and still be a kid in the process. Not get caught up in the day-to-day drudgery of life in the city."

She leaned in and pressed a soft kiss to his mouth. Inching backward, she whispered, "You're a great dad." Her finger slid down the dusting of stubble on his chin.

He turned and kissed it. "Thanks for the vote of confidence."

"Elaine doesn't know what she's missing."

The weight of her words felt important. Like she was implying so much more, and he loved it. "Come on, Sunshine, outside." He grabbed her hand. "The dishes can wait. Time for that surprise I mentioned."

A squeal was the only response he got as Sunny's fingers escaped from his, and she sped toward the door.

****

The winter scene pumped Noah with excess energy, anticipating with childlike abandon his first ride down Collision Hill all season. Not with his kids this time but with Sunny wrapped up tight, snug in his arms. The thought heated him to his core. "When's the last time you went sledding?"

"A while back. My college days I think." Staring down at the brand-new Flexible Flyer sled, complete with red steel runners, that he'd managed to find in town—the only one left in town—she shifted her feet back and forth, digging a path into the packed snow. Her gaze shot to the sky. "I could just watch from here and enjoy the view. It's pretty. Peaceful, with the snow drifting down."

"Peaceful? With the kids whooping and hollering…parents screaming… Not sure I agree with you there. Plus the ride is meant to be exhilarating."

She shrugged, focusing on the pile of people clambering from the latest collision at the bottom of the hill.

"Look. It may have been a couple years, but your muscles will remember. Climb on. Prepare yourself for an epic thrill." A hint of fear crept into her eyes, so he kept talking. "You won't regret it. I promise. Just hang on, and I'll keep you safe. Deal?"

"Deal," she breathed out, and that fear transformed, her hazel eyes taking on a glint of steel.

He'd witnessed it before when they were discussing her business plan for *Endeavor*. Determination. "Okay. Settle in. I'll give us a push and jump on behind you. I'll help you steer, or you can—"

"Just hurry up, before I lose my nerve."

"Yes, ma'am." One step and another and they were off. Noah anchored into place behind her, helping to guide the shaking sled, picking up speed, barreling down the hill under their weight, racing faster…faster.

Sunny screamed, adding to the din of the crowd, as the world blurred by in a sea of white.

Burrowing close into her neck, he murmured, "Feel that thrill? Nothing quite like it…"

"Look," she stammered. "Ahead, don't hit them."

He grabbed the reins. "I've got it," he yelled. *I hope*… But they were coming in too fast… He held his breath and slung one arm around her, bracing them both.

In the nick of time, they swerved slightly right, slowing, before their sled toppled over.

"Are you okay?"

"Sure. Can we go again? Now?"

"You bet." He chuckled. Dragging the sled behind him, he swung her around in a small circle so she ended up tucked next to him. "Did you feel that? I could have sworn something nudged us out of the way of those people, huddled at the end of the line, right at the last second. We almost cut right into them."

"No…not really. Too caught up in the moment, I guess."

He had felt their momentum shift. Thank goodness too. He'd sensed her hesitation just now before she answered him. His perception of human nature was excellent. A tool he honed daily in his business dealings. People told a lot about themselves, when given the chance, through the subtleties of their body language and the intonations in their voices. So why was she ignoring the truth?

They stayed out on that hill for hours, traipsing up, sledding down again, mingling with kids and their parents. As the afternoon wore on, Noah called it. "Let's get you home. My surprises for the day aren't done, and you need to warm up before we take one more trek in the snow this afternoon."

Her eyebrows lifted, and he moved in, taking her by surprise, kissing the chill from her lips as they curved upward.

****

Their afternoon ended with Noah playing mountain man, chopping down a Christmas tree for her at the local tree farm. "You don't have time, with moving in and your new business that needs attention. Since the kids are spending the next few weeks at their mother's, I don't have anyone to share my Christmas spirit with." He flashed her a broad, heart-stopping smile, dropped the ax to the ground, his arms open in a shrug.

Sunny ran and jumped into them. "Thank you for sharing your spirit with me."

"There's nowhere else I'd rather be," he said, his voice hoarse in her ear.

She meant what she said about the spirit emanating from him. Noah's aura drew her toward him. No mistaking it. This was more than a passing attraction. They had a bond—deeper, stronger than any physical attraction. She hadn't experienced this before. Ever.

Layer upon layer, forces were knitting them together.

They put up the tree, Noah following her guidance, moving it this way, then the other, until it stood perfectly. Again he brought out presents from his trunk—decorations, lights. "Well, you can't have a tree trimming without the trimmings, right?"

"You're amazing… Anything else hidden in there?"

He gave her an all-knowing grin. "You'll just have to wait and see."

"I'm so grateful. I haven't had a day like this in, well…never."

Swirling white coated the grass, trees, mailboxes, and road, their entire world hidden in a blanket of snow. When a tapping sound began outside, the tiny little shards hitting the roof and windows, Noah perked up from the pot he was stirring. "It's ice." His brows furrowed. "I'll dish up the vegetable stew, and we'll eat. Then I should go. The roads will be impassable soon if they're not already."

Heat spilled into the room from the fingers of fire Sunny had suddenly conjured up, the Christmas lights twinkling from her final touches. She'd lost count of the spells she interjected here and there throughout the day. Stopping wasn't really an option; to her the magic she spun came as naturally as breathing.

But soon they needed to have a more formal conversation. Humans generally freaked about this part of her. Sunny lifted up a silent prayer that Noah wouldn't be one of those. Her magical presence couldn't be altered. Dread wasn't too strong a word for how she felt about summoning the courage to tell him about this part of her.

Their gazes connected, his drilling into hers, as she

joined him at the stove. "Don't go," she mouthed, taking his free hand. "A man who cooks after a full day out in the snow, then tree trimming? You are a rarity, Mr. Russell."

Noah's lips quirked up. "I've enjoyed all of it." His gaze dropped, scrutinizing where his fingers grazed hers. "But I want to make something clear. You don't owe me anything."

"I…I didn't mean…" The power flickered, on, off, then on again.

"Uh-oh. Here it comes… And off again. I was expecting that. Good thing dinner is hot."

"Noah, I don't feel that I owe you."

"Okay. Just putting it out there." He waved her to the table to eat. The fire provided plenty of light, and they could take their time if he didn't have to leave. Once they finished their meal, he scooted his chair back and carried their bowls to the sink.

"Come on," she said. "Let's keep warm by the fire where we can see better. The dishes can wait."

Hand in hand, the two sank into the cushions piled on the floor.

"What a peaceful, cozy end to your surprise-filled day."

He pressed a kiss to her forehead. "I'm glad you enjoyed it. I'll remember today always—your expressions…your joy," he finished.

The silence stretched, the crackling, hissing fire and howling wind filling the space between them.

"What is it? I can almost hear your gears working, Noah."

"Yeah, I'm like that sometimes. In my head a lot. Elaine hated that about me."

"Well, I don't. If you want to share whatever it is, I'm here. But I get it. I'm the same way. I don't like to talk about what's still brewing inside me."

"That's the thing. I've decided." He leveled her with his gaze. "I'm pulling back to focus on the charity arm of my business, the James Russell Foundation. I've given it thought off and on for the past month. My center of operations would be here. Not in the city. Of course I'd travel back and forth for meetings and events. Those would be my focus."

He shook his head. "I can't deny it anymore. The resources the foundation will gather can offer hope to so many. I want to spend my time honoring my brother's memory while creating a home base for my kids to return to…*here*. Feels good to finally say it out loud. What do you think?"

She leaped into his lap. "Noah, that's so exciting! I'm so proud of you. All of your success culminating to fulfill your dream. A dream that will connect with and heal others."

"Yeah?"

"Yeah."

He pressed their bodies together, his mouth finding hers. She opened for him, and their tongues danced, exploring, searching.

"Sunshine, I should leave," he panted.

"No. It's not safe out there."

"What about in here? Do you feel safe, Sunny?"

"Yes. Very."

"Tell me to go."

"Stay," she whispered, closing the distance between them again.

"Are you sure?"

In the dim light, the flames flickered, punctuating the stillness with their heat.

"Yes, Noah."

His fingers anchored in her hair. "You're magnificent."

His gaze pinning her, her heart stuttering under his adoration, she murmured, "Don't make me wait any longer."

"You have no idea what those words do to me. If you did—"

"*Shh*. Show me."

****

Noah woke on the floor of the living room, amid cushions and quilts, near the fireplace, to an odd energy surrounding him, one he'd experienced yesterday off and on. He couldn't quite put his finger on it. Maybe today would be different. But the intensity seemed stronger, closer. Stretching his arms, he reached for Sunny. The covers had gone cold where her body had been snuggled next to his. Last night had been magical when they surrendered to each other, fulfilling parts of him that had been aching for a long time. She was his answer. He'd tell her so this morning.

Fire sizzled and snapped behind the grate, the coffeepot gurgling in the background. A satisfied smile rose on his lips. *Power's back on. Thank God.* Yanking on pants, he hopped one-legged toward the kitchen and scanned for Sunny… He blinked. *What the hell?* Pots and pans from last night's dinner slithered back and forth under the water, completely of their own volition, before slipping precariously into the drainer.

On the stove, what appeared to be a fried egg hung inexplicably in midair, suspended for a two count, before flipping over and hitting the hot pan again with a long slow hiss. His smile evaporated. *I must be dreaming.*

Then, staring wide-eyed, he turned full circle, studying the situation, his mouth moving in silent incomprehension, willing the scene to make some kind of sense.

"You were sound asleep," Sunny said. "I…I was only gone a minute." A loud clatter sounded, as dishes and plates fell to the sink, the odor of burning eggs filling the air.

"Sunny, I'm a man of facts, of numbers, of reason." He gestured with both hands. "So please, explain this to me in a way I can understand."

Her chest rose with her deep breath. "I…I'm a witch, Noah."

His eyes narrowed and refocused. "Come again?"

"You heard me."

"No. I don't think I did. 'Cause the woman I'm falling in love with just told me that she's a witch. I must have a screw loose somewhere."

"*Love?*"

"Love," he repeated, dropping onto a kitchen barstool.

"It's really not a big deal," she began.

He glanced at the sink filled with dirty dishes. Wasn't the *big deal* in the room proven without any additional clarification? "That's why you didn't mention it?"

"This, your reaction right now, is why I didn't mention it sooner."

He growled his next words as they spewed from his mouth. "When, exactly, would you have deemed it significant enough to bring up?"

"Today." She lifted her head a little higher. "*Love*?"

"*Love*." His mouth formed a straight line. "Sit for a minute. Please." He heaved a deep breath of his own. "To totally clear the air, you need to know *One Perfect Life* is mine. I—well, Russell Enterprises—acquired it. Who the hell came up with that awful name by the way? Never mind… Point is, I should have told you sooner. I've never experienced these feelings before, surrounding a business deal. Never had any question or hesitation," he clarified. "And watching you rise to the occasion, develop your own business, seize the moment—I'm so proud of you. It's…disconcerting, my concern for your welfare—"

His Sunshine froze for a second, and it tore him apart the moment all the pieces clicked together.

"Oh, I get it now. That's why all the attention. To make yourself feel better because you feel sorry for me. I don't need your pity."

"No, Sunny. No! My feelings for you are separate and apart from the mechanics of the business deal." He rubbed his temples. "I can't explain it, beyond that I feel like we're meant to be together despite the obstacles thrown in our way."

"I need some…distance, Noah." Tiny golden sparks escaped from her fingertips, like she had contained her power just barely, with a waning constraint that could abandon her at any moment.

He watched in awe, different scenarios from their time together replaying in his thoughts, becoming clearer with this new knowledge. "I agree." He bowed his head, scrounging together what was left of his floundering composure. "For now, that might be best." He grasped her hand that, mere seconds ago, had been infused with light and yanked her close. "Last night was…frankly—" He sighed. "—I don't have the words, Sunshine." He kissed her slow and soft. Inside, his heart thundered, needy…hungry…for another taste of her.

Instead he took her at her word and pulled back, pressed a lingering kiss on her hand, then shrugged on his sweater, grabbed his coat, kicked his feet into his boots, and left without another word.

****

Five days had passed and nothing from Noah. Day after tomorrow was Christmas Eve; after that, the following week would be his benefit. Was this it? The end of the road for them? Sunny's time with him had made her feel alive, like no other relationship had in the past. It sounded stupid, but she believed she held a part of his soul within hers, and she always would because of what they'd shared, despite what might or might not happen in the future. They'd experienced a deep connection, and during the days they'd been apart, it had grown stronger, not lessened.

Sunny had retrieved her grandmother's necklace from the nightstand and worn it since the day Noah had left, hoping to glean something of importance. Gripping the small gem hanging from her neck, she wondered about its place in all this. Beyond the pulsing and magic exuding from the jewelry, nothing specific or remarkable had happened—yet. But she was far from giving up.

Enchanted pieces of art worked in tandem with other magic derived from the basic elements, constantly weaving, spinning, leading to outcomes no one could predict. For now, she'd keep the faith. In Noah. In what they'd found together.

Sunny's excess worries and energy found a home.

And today, like the last five, she poured them into her business. Preliminary announcements had gone out to all subscribers, and another would be forthcoming the last week of the month, showcasing what *Endeavor*'s first issue would highlight.

Since her initial issue would arrive inside in-boxes during the first full week of the coming year, she'd decided to focus on beginnings. The main thrust of this installment would fall under Going Green, how to begin and keep the momentum going. This headlining article would ease one into the process, and, going forward, Sunny had planned a column with additional pointers and strategies for the average person to adopt, without breaking the budget, along with additional options to help adapt long term and to stick to their go-green choice.

Other bits included a piece on organic gardening, where and how to begin, as well as locations of where one could find farms that utilized these techniques in growing their products. Products and companies she endorsed, when they appeared in the magazine, would be documented, with links connected to verifiable research. These goods or services would receive the *Endeavor* seal of recommendation—a sun rising, which was also her new logo… He didn't know it, but Noah had inspired this graphic update with his nickname for her—Sunshine—and she loved the look. Fitting for her fresh start.

The research and actual writing of the articles had taken place months ago. Organizing and adding the last-minute touches ignited her growing passion in her work. Some would like what she had to offer; others would not. Finding her tribe wouldn't be easy, but she would; then she'd find other like-minded folks and grow her subscriber base. A market segment, hungry for her information, existed, and she would meet that need in abundance. Then repeat and wait for a verdict.

Beside her, Sunny's phone lit with a text. Noah…

—Sorry I've gone dark. Had a lot to work through. I'd like to talk to you about it if you'll let me. Christmas Eve is two days away. Would you meet me?—

Christmas… His decorations surrounded her. Her gaze perused the festive tree, trimmed with ornaments and strung with sparkling lights. He had wrapped her in reminders that the holiday was closing in fast. Seen to it that the coming celebration would include her and her rundown house, since she'd been covered up in work and boxes from the move, not to mention the added stress from being let go from work. He'd seen to many of her needs. Because of guilt? His words echoed through her thoughts. *The woman I'm falling in love with*. That conversation had repeated over and over in her head, and the ending never changed.

—I've been busy finalizing my first issue. But I could use a distraction. Where? When?—

Her knee bobbed up and down as she waited for his response. Maybe he'd changed his mind after reflecting over their whirlwind of time together. Maybe he'd decided love was too strong of a word for his feelings. If so, this meeting would just be his polite way of letting her down easy.

—Be sure to add me to your subscriber list. I'd like to receive your inaugural issue and every one after that. Let's meet on Christmas Eve, an hour after sundown, at the ice-skating rink in the town square. What's your size? I'm guessing about a seven.—

Skating? *Ugh*…

—Seven and a half. I haven't skated since my teenage years. I'll make a fool of myself.—

—Christmas is a magical time. (Heart emoji) I'm sure you'll make the best of it. (Sorry, I couldn't resist.)—

—I'll be there. See you soon.—

—Thank goodness. I thought I'd have to grovel, beg...—

—Don't discount that possibility. (Grinning emoji)—

—God, I've missed you. (Sad face emoji)—

Yes… She let out her pent-up breath.

—Me too.—

****

Noah arrived early. Christmas Eve was by far his favorite day of the holidays. Because the anticipation hanging over the day was so tantalizing, so palpable, so real for him, it trumped the actual day itself. Typically gifts had been purchased, or not, kids on their best behavior, the refrigerator overflowing with seasonal favorites, specialty drinks close at hand, his ex-wife too busy with this or that to bother with him. And work? His ever-present motivator and savior? On idle for a short time. So he reveled in the waiting. Watching the night unfold, knowing that the excitement couldn't be exceeded on this most special of nights. The night of promise for what was to come.

He'd taken a quick trip into the city. To make a pit stop in Russell Enterprises headquarters, to shake hands all around, have the requisite drink with his upper management staff, to hand out Christmas bonuses, but mostly for the purchase of a special gift. Here in Willingham Creek they didn't have one of these in the local shops.

Wrapping his fingers around the little black box with its tiny red bow, he envisioned the contents—a stunning but tasteful diamond-studded bracelet. Something his Sunshine could wear around town if she chose. Beginning today, he'd shower her with diamonds. And in April, her birthday month, he'd ask the woman of his dreams to marry him, and what a rock he'd dazzle her with then. That was, if tonight went according to plan.

The night they spent together, followed by the morning of revelation, had been a shock. Spending the better part of that next day thinking of the time they had passed together, he came to the realization that his soul had found its mate and that he would spend the rest of his time here on Earth convincing Sunny of that fact. Whatever it took. Beginning tonight on the magical evening of Christmas Eve.

So as of this week, he'd added another bucket to his system: Sunny, kids, business. The shake-up clicked right into place with her love surrounding him.

Witchcraft, he had to admit, had him wary. But that, he realized, with a few days of perspective, was only another aspect of what made his Sunshine unique and precious. Plus, any children who might result from their union, and he hoped for them one day in the not-too-distant future, would also potentially be part witch. And damn…that was more than okay. *I'm all in.*

With the help of Alex, the initial draft of his speech for next week's event had been completed several days ago. Noah had tweaked it and made it his own. At this charity event, he planned to announce the decision that he'd only unveiled to Sunny and, as of yesterday, to Alex as well. The most profound relief had filtered through him when he made it official. And in the flash of his thoughts, his brother's image materialized, his face proud, smiling, that—along with Sunny's—the only validation Noah needed.

Children spun and twisted their limbs tight in the air, landing on the perfect edge of their skates. The rink was full tonight. He couldn't help but think of Janie and Rob and how they might react to the impending changes in his life. He'd help them adapt. His instincts told Noah that his kids would love Sunny too. Eventually he'd want the two of them here with him and Sunny. The life he'd been working toward for so long… He was right on the cusp. The anticipation swept through him, crisp…sweet… He could practically taste it.

The scent of her perfume reached him a few seconds before she did. Sunny kissed him on the side of his neck, beginning a sensation that cascaded warmth throughout his entire body. "Sunshine, thanks for coming."

Just like that, his wait skidded to a halt. She wore a cute red pullover cap, accented with an adorable green puff ball that bobbled when she walked. Her jeans clung tight to her muscled calves, and peeking out from her coat shone a tiny light from what had to be Rudolph.

"You look incredible. I'm guessing that Rudolph under there has your own special touch added in."

She shook her head. "Just batteries. Found it at the Save and Shop today, on sale. It's breathtaking, by the way, all of this. I'd be okay with just watching from here. I bought us some hot chocolate from Cora on the way in. She set up a booth. I couldn't resist." She offered him a steaming cup, then scooted in beside him.

"So good," he said after taking a sip. "Warm yourself up before we take a spin in a few minutes. I, uh, brought you a few things. I won't see you tomorrow, most likely. My day will include on and off appearances, via video chat with my kids, then later a quick meeting with Alex."

"On Christmas?" she interrupted.

"Yes, a short business meeting. Alex asked for it before she heads this way for the event. She'll be off the two days between Christmas and then, so she wanted to preempt any loose ends beforehand."

"Noah, I'm sorry about everything," she began in a rush of breath. "I'm used to people cutting and running when they find out about me. The few who know, that is. At first I just thought we'd be acquaintances, and although grateful for your help when I moved in, I imagined we'd see very little of each other."

"Little of each other…in Willingham Creek?"

"You know what I mean."

A smirk crossed his face. "I think I do, yes. I, on the contrary, had plans to see a lot of you, and when I found out about your predicament, indirectly caused by me, I felt horrible. But later, after I reviewed your plan, my concerns eased. Success is right around the corner for you, Sunny. I truly believe it."

"I hope you're right."

"I am." He cocked his head. "Still, I should have told you about my connection with the magazine on our first date. I have no excuse other than I didn't want you to ditch me before giving us a chance."

"I understand. Your instincts were right. But what now? I'm still a witch. I won't pretend I'm not. I won't fault you, Noah, for moving on. You have your foundation to consider, not to mention your kids. You could have anyone you want."

"Stop right there."

"But I'm on a roll, and I'm afraid I won't get this out before…"

"It's time for my surprises." He grinned.

"You mean skates? I'm going to plaster my face on the ice. *Can't wait*."

"Your own pair of skates was my first surprise. We'll go out together. I won't let go until you're ready. I promise."

"You have another surprise?"

He nodded as she watched him produce the black box with the cheery red ribbon. "Merry Christmas." He leaned in and pressed his lips against hers. "Open it."

With a gentle tug, the ribbon floated free. Gasping at the first sight of diamonds, she froze, her eyes widening. "Noah, it's amazing, but I can't—"

"Nope. No buts." He loosened the bracelet from the box and fastened the latch around her wrist. "Beautiful," he announced, admiring the jewelry.

"Noah…I'm stunned. I don't know what to say."

"Then let me." He took her hands in his. "I love you, Sunny. You truly have become my Sunshine—essential to me, like air. I need you in my life, and I'll make that request official very soon."

"What? But I'm a…"

"Witch. Yes. That's had time to sink in now. And you're perfect just as you are. I'm not sure what it all means yet, but I'd like for you to teach me. Would you?"

"Yes. We'll go slow and easy. So you can keep up."

She winked, and the promise implied in her words had him gritting his teeth. "I like the sound of that. Before you turn me into a groveling mess, will you take a spin with me on the ice?"

"After all this?" The wonder in her eyes made his surprises worth it, just to capture this moment with her. "Yes, Mr. Russell."

He passed her the other festively wrapped gift and kissed her nose. "Slip them on, Sunshine, and let's go."

After several spins around the rink, he gave her an appraising glance. "What did I tell you? Look at you go. It's all coming back. Just like a bicycle."

"Not true—"

Her arms pinwheeled, her balance compromised by a kid who'd clipped her, whizzing by, showing off. Noah maneuvered his body between Sunny and the ice as she faltered. Laughing uncontrollably, in a tangle of arms and legs, they went down.

****

Going Sunnyless wasn't an option. Hadn't been since the day he'd assaulted her with his coffee cup. A slow grin overtook his face as he watched her, deep in concentration, bent over her laptop, proofing her very first issue. All the ingredients were there to make her *Endeavor* a success: drive, determination, brains, creativity. If he'd met her earlier, he'd have hired her himself. Instead of, well, firing her. But the alternative—this—was so much sweeter.

They'd spent the last two nights wrapped around each other, the after-Christmas haze melting in the slow, easy time they enjoyed together. Noah reveled in each second, overcome with each new discovery, every nuance inherent within the woman he loved sliding into place.

Everything was a go for tomorrow's event, the beginning of his new focus—the James Russell Foundation. In between tweaking the final version of his

51

speech, he'd offered Sunny advice on life as an entrepreneur, not as the corporate mogul Noah Russell, but just as her confidant and lover. "Sunshine, you're gonna crush this. My instincts are rarely wrong."

Her lips curved up, her eyelashes sweeping down, the combination of the two seizing his attention. The buzzer sounded. She slid from her barstool and pulled the pan of cookies from the oven. While the current batch cooled, she attended to another; with a twitch of her wrist, the delectable caramel drizzled over the tiny creations. The pecan pieces came next, prancing in a line, the sparkle of her magic circling the entire operation.

Noah snatched one of the finished cookies, piled high with caramel, pecans, and a dusting of sugar. The first bite melted in his mouth. He groaned. "I never eat stuff like this, except when I'm reading at Books and Treasures, but Cora's pastries can't touch this little slice of heaven." He dipped the last bite into his coffee and swallowed it. "I have another idea if you're up for it."

She laughed, a light joyful sound from atop her perch, already deep into her proofs again. "Stop eating the cookies, Noah, or we won't have enough to serve the guests tomorrow."

"I'm not worried about that. The event's fully catered. The ones lucky enough to have a taste of these won't forget them. Perfect segue to my point."

She dragged her gaze to meet his.

"What would you think about selling these delicious treats to bakeries, restaurants, coffee shops, then from there—"

"Noah, stop. Turn off your brain for a minute. I don't want to sell these. They're special, a legacy from my grandmother. I feel her presence whenever I bake them. I don't want them to be shot out from some cold, speedy assembly line. They'd be missing a couple ingredients that machines could never replicate—the infusion of bits of magic and, of course, love."

"Understood." He whispered in her ear, snaking his arms around her waist. "I'll always be an eager recipient, taste tester, whatever you need."

She turned in his arms. "You've given me everything, right here."

She inched closer, and he gave in to the urge as he paused, inhaling the essence of his Sunshine. And when her lips moved with his, he basked in her rays of warmth…basked in her love…basked in what the two of them were together. Two hearts finding each other.

****

Sunny clapped along with the large crowd gathered outside in the gardens surrounding city hall. Her gaze traveled Noah's fine muscled form, clad in a gray flannel business suit. His open coat allowed for an unobstructed view, and while she loved him casual with jeans slung low on his hips, this side of him, working the crowd, was off-the-charts hot too.

Within moments he'd had the audience enthralled, putty in his hands, while he relayed a story of James and him as kids, creating mischief and having fun. She'd heard his speech yesterday, but here, with a live crowd, was another thing entirely. The emotion, the grit, and pain of the loss all translated seamlessly to his eager audience. The wind cleared the tears from her cheeks. Noah had made the right choice, following his heart.

He waved her over to where he greeted his family, pumping hands one second, then snatching his youngest, Rob, as he'd hurtled himself into his dad's arms.

"Elaine." Noah forced a smile, accompanying the tight nod of his head. "Thanks for bringing the kids."

"No problem. I still enjoy watching the effect you have on a crowd. Mesmerizing." She cleared her throat. "They have plenty of pent-up energy from Christmas. Good luck with that." She flashed a practiced smile that fell from her face when her gaze met Sunny's.

"Oh, we've got plans for them." Noah turned to his children. "Go inside. Have a *few* refreshments and warm up." He pushed them toward the door. "Elaine, I'd like you to meet my girlfriend, soon to be fiancée if she'll have me."

"Nice to meet you." Sunny offered her hand.

"How many does that make since the divorce, Noah?"

He let her snide comment die a cold lonely death in the wind as the woman offered a limp hand that Sunny gripped firmly, then released. "Enjoy all this," Elaine spouted out. "This tiny little town was never my thing. But Noah's always thrived here. I'm guessing you're the same?"

Sunny attempted to hold back her laughter, a few seconds later losing the battle. Noah's gaze shot to hers.

"Oh, Willingham Creek is most definitely my thing."

"Ours," he corrected, tucking her to his side. "How about a drink and one of your cookies, Sunshine?"

"I'd love it."

He laced their fingers together. "I'll talk to you on the second to arrange pickup, Elaine," he added over his shoulder, leaving her alone in the snow, her mouth gaping open.

Poor woman, Sunny decided, to let go of man like

Noah. And for what? Glitz, stuff, status? At his core her man was so much more. Passion, strength, integrity, determination, and, of course, love flowed from the man snuggled beside her, and she had experienced every one of those traits in abundance with him. Elaine had had her chance and lost out. Sunny turned her gaze to meet the simmering pools of his eyes.

"Where did you go just then?"

"Just thinking about how lucky I am."

He pressed a kiss to her forehead, a soft sigh escaping from him. "No…I'm the lucky one, smashing that coffee into you, bringing your sunshine into my dreary life. I'm done for." He squeezed her hand and covered her mouth with his, plucking gently at her lips. "You're everything to me, Sunshine."

****

Was this really her life? Sunny paused, pressed up onto her toes, and kissed Noah. Just because she could.

He smiled against her lips. "Your cookies were a hit. Only crumbs left after the first fifteen minutes."

"Your event was the hit. I can't wait to hear how much money you raised."

"I hope you're right. It felt good today, releasing information to the public about where I'm headed, what my focus will be going forward."

Sunny leaned into Noah, making it hard for her to mentally switch gears.

"Ready for the storm that is my kids? Picking up…dropping off…it's a never-ending battle." He opened the door to his SUV and assisted her inside. "But it's easier this way, today with separate cars." A twinge of irritation trickled into his voice. "I had no idea how much the kids had brought. They'll meet us at my place.

Only one transfer of stuff. From the sounds of it, they both have multiple suitcases and other accessories." He rolled his eyes. "They pack like their mother."

"No problem."

He slammed the door shut and turned over the motor.

"She misses what you once had. I could tell. It's written all over her face. I kinda feel sorry for her."

His lips quirked. "Don't. She made out fine in the divorce. Cash is what she likes, not me, not any longer."

"That's not what I saw deep in her eyes today."

"Stop. You're gonna make me gag. Can you hand me my gloves from the glove compartment?"

"Sure." She gave the handle a yank and watched all the contents of the small space spill forward into her lap. "You've got a little of everything in here," she teased, digging. "First aid supplies, napkins, straws, jelly beans, gum, acetaminophen."

"What can I say?" He shrugged. "*Kids*."

"Here they are, gloves."

"Thanks."

"Wait, what's this?" Her mouth opened, her heart skipping a beat, recognition shooting through her.

"Oh, a key ring. My grandfather gave it to me." He chuckled. "I don't remember how long ago. He made me promise to always keep it with me. So I move it from car to car. I'd never break my word to him. For some reason it was important to him. The only clue he gave me about his gift was that someday I'd understand. I believed him."

She pulled out her necklace, warm from her skin where it had lain under the layers of her shirt and sweater. "A match," she said low, trailing her fingers along the stone embedded in the key ring.

Worry lines creased his forehead. "What's wrong, honey?"

"This is a cat's-eye opal." A shiver skittered across her skin. "Witch lore states that the stone would find its mate and the wearers would be destined to be lifelong partners."

As he studied the gems, Noah's mouth spread into a face-splitting grin. "And you're the one surprised here, Sunshine? I say, hell yeah!"

"I…I'd kinda given up on it, you know?" For the second time today, a tear drifted down her cheek. "I got mine a long time ago when I was sixteen."

"Some things are worth the wait. Like the feeling I have when my kids are here, like finding the perfect point in time to center my focus on the foundation, like everything falling in place for you in my life… Come here, gorgeous." He kissed the surprise from her lips. "Like the realization that my favorite place on Earth finally means *home* again."

Spritz Cookie Showdown

by

Melanie Hoffer

Christmas Cookies

Dedication

To my mother.
I couldn't have done this without you.

.

Chapter One

After baking five trays of my specialty Christmas cookie, all I want to do is crawl back into bed. Not tonight, though. I opened my big mouth and RSVP'd to my unofficial ten-year high school reunion. The extra icing on the cake is the theme. An ugly sweater party with a Christmas cookie competition. *The party better have strong drinks.*

The sweet aroma of freshly baked spritz cookies wafts through the kitchen. I inhale the delicious air and smile. I scoop up the last batch, green Christmas trees with red sprinkles and layer them into the last holiday tin. I only need thirty cookies for the contest, but they are getting all fifty of them whether they like it or not.

"Don't forget to soak the cookie press in warm water and take the metal discs out of the sink," my mother adds from her spot at the kitchen table. She peeks over the mound of wrapped Christmas presents, inspecting my cleanup.

I sigh. "The cookie press is in the sink, and I already washed the discs. They are in the box over there." I point over at the drying tray.

"All right, just making sure, Tara. Two of the discs rusted the last time you made these." Her eyebrow rises.

"Yes, mom." I close my eyes, resisting the flood of painful memories about the last time. Irritation still furrows my brow. My mother just casually brings up the day my last boyfriend broke up with me as if I forgot to pick up her dry cleaning. The day in question is the exact reason why I'm here in my parents' kitchen using the potholders I made my mom in my fifth-grade art class. Six months living back at home drags on forever.

I roll my shoulders back and shake out my hands. Pleasant thoughts: Unicorns, hot bubble baths, sloth videos on the internet. Tonight is not about my ex. I will show my face at the party, win the cookie war, and get the hell out of there. Easy enough unless a certain person graces us all with his presence.

"I wonder if Shane Brooks is going to be there? He might want some cookie revenge if he still has all of his hair?" my mother jokes.

"Mom, please! You're making me nervous enough as it is," I shout. Shane's hair is intact and has the perfect, sexy flop over his forehead. I must stop stalking him on social media before I lose my mind.

"I'm sorry, forget I brought him up." My mom waves her hand in front of her face.

"If he shows up, I will shove a tin of cookies in his face and watch him eat my victory."

"Why would he miss it? He used to be best friends with the popular girls. They're throwing this party, right?"

My mother means well, but her poking and prodding are making my current living situation worse.

I whip around to steer the conversation elsewhere, especially off Shane Brooks, and the last cookie on my snowflake spatula goes flying onto the floor. Our German Shepard wastes no time shuffling into the kitchen and snatching up the runaway cookie. I pinch the bridge of my nose. His happy smile at my sugary treat warms me back down. My mother groans in the background.

"Please turn the *Days we haven't dropped food for Mickey* counter back to zero days. I made that sign for a reason. We all have to use it."

"Yes, mom." For a second, guilt overcomes me because the sign read sixty days. *Oh, well.* I flip the numbers back to zero, beginning the countdown again.

My checklist is almost complete. Without any further distractions, including furry kinds, I have an hour left for my makeup, my hair, and putting on the ugly sweater I borrowed from my best friend. A drunken reindeer with Christmas lights hooked around his antlers is flipping off Santa and Rudolph while holding a sequined covered beer in his other hand. I laughed so hard when Danielle wore it two years ago. Luckily, it fits me too.

I escape my mother and run upstairs. My childhood bedroom is the last door on the left. The lock has been broken since I slammed the door extra hard one day in highschool. Shane Brooks ruined that day and my first kiss. *Damn him.*

What if he shows up at the party? My lips tingle, remembering his kiss even after all this time. First kisses are supposed to be unsure, sloppy, and wet, but that was never Shane's style. His expertise blew me away and turned my legs to jelly. I drowned in his kiss as we made out against a cold, metal pole underneath the bleachers. He stirred my lust from the depths of my soul and imagination. Then, he took it all away.

He refused to eat one of my spritz cookies after I won the cookie challenge in home economics the day after we kissed. Shane never forgave me for winning and getting a well-deserved A from Mrs. Musso. He also started dating Amber Reed later that afternoon.

My mother knocks on the doorjamb to my room. "Have a great time tonight, hunny. You're going to look hilarious."

"Thanks, I think." I roll my eyes.

"You'll be fine. By the way, I texted Shane's mom. She said he is going to the party. He has been home for a few weeks because of a bad break-up. Now you have something in common with him!"

"Mom!" I yell, dropping the contents of my makeup bag onto the floor.

At least my mother can read between the lines of my death stare. She whispers an apology and shuts my door.

I kneel and throw my scattered makeup back into the bag. My gaze gravitates toward the crossed-out section on my old bulletin board hanging on the back of my door. There used to be hearts around Shane's name. I drew over a hundred of them the night he kissed me. The next day, I used my black eyeliner, then a permanent marker, and made all those hearts disappear.

Shane's attendance changes everything about tonight, and I will be stuck wearing an ugly sweater listening to a crap ton of 'How have you been for the past ten years' game on repeat. I only want to hear stories from him and then slap him in the face for giving me the best kiss of my life.

He better show up tonight. We have unfinished business.

Chapter Two

A line of cars wraps around the block in front of the gorgeous mansion belonging to Stephanie Myerson's parents. I park on the next street over at the first stretch of open curb. The night's crisp air is extra cold for December, but I pick up my four cookie tins from the passenger seat and make my way through the cars.

After the brisk walk to the house, I pause on the cobblestone walkway and survey the scene. All the curtains are open, granting me a peek at the ugly sweater horror. At least, this is not the big, official high school reunion happening after Christmas. This is an invitation-only snooze fest for the popular kids, but Shane will be here.

He belongs in this crowd. I was never popular and always left out of the cool kid parties. One time I got invited to one of Stephanie's infamous nights, but it was the Track team party. The coach probably made her do it.

I shake away the sense of dread creeping up my spine. This is only a party. I know all the dirt about these people thanks to social media and Melissa, the Gossip Queen, whom I keep running into at the supermarket. I try avoiding her, but without fail, she finds me. A few weeks ago, she followed me around long enough to mention the party and offer me an invitation. I said yes too fast, sealing my fate.

Let's get this done already.

I hit the doorbell with my elbow, and the gossip queen opens the front door a second later. Her hot pink lips stretch wide as she announces my arrival. *I should have stayed in the car.*

"Everyone, Ms. Cookie Winner is here! Should I just give her the prize now?" she shouts over the music.

To my demise, all the people in the foyer and adjoining dining room turn toward the door, checking me out from head to toe. I recognize everyone as I scan the people in front of me. Their fake, polite smiles happen all at once. I step back, losing my balance, and the two top cookie tins slip off my stack from my trembling hands. A blur of a man rushes over, catching the tins before they hit the ground.

I smell him before I drag my gaze up the chest of the man plaguing my every thought. His cologne welcomes me, tempting me further. If I don't look at his face, it might not be him wearing a white sweater with a sloth dressed up as Santa Claus on the front, holding a sign: *Ugly Sweater Stand-in.*

"You have to be more careful, Tara. You wouldn't want to mess up your losing cookies now, would you?" Shane says over my head.

It's him. I bite my bottom lip and look up. His eyes are still the color of cherry wood, and his smirk of kissable, full lips makes me speechless. His goatee hides his baby face, but when he throws back his head, laughing, he looks like he has not aged at all.

Wait, did he say losing cookies?

I grab my tins back from his hands.

"Um, shouldn't we at least say hello before throwing cheap shots at each other?" I retort.

"Hello there. I should have let them fall if we are going to play that game. Can we hug and make up?" He spreads his arms out, the Christmas sloth mimicking his movement, and continues smiling.

I swear I remember him being sweet, funny, romantic, and an over-the-top gentleman. *Where the hell did that guy go?* This guy is a dick.

A sigh of relief falls from my mouth. I dodged this bullet.

"Now, Shane, you promised me you would fight fair and let everyone try all the other contestants' cookies. Don't sabotage Tara," Stephanie, the hostess says. She appears at the top of the grand staircase in the entryway. All eyes fixate on her, just like in high school, as she walks down the stairs like a runway model. Her ugly sweater dress is adorable and not ugly at all. Like Shane, there is a wide-eyed Christmas sloth on the front holding a candy cane. She walks up to Shane and drapes her hands over his broad shoulders. Even though she is wearing at least three-inch heels, she still leans up to kiss Shane's half-shaven cheek.

They are quite cozy in front of everyone. Shane's hand loops around her lower back as she whispers something behind her manicured hand. The candy cane stripes on her fingernails sparkle when she giggles up at Shane.

My shock wears off, and I close my gaping mouth. I'm not surprised Shane is already taken by Stephanie. In our senior year, they won almost every superlative; best looking, best cars, and even best friends forever. *I guess they found each other again.*

A gust of cold air ruffles my hair, reminding me the front door remains wide open. I've been here less than two minutes, barely over the mistletoe threshold, and my worst nightmare is playing out in front of me. I contemplate walking right back to my car. However, the possibility of revenge against Shane makes me shut the door and face the night ahead.

Chapter Three

Without looking back at Shane and Stephanie, I head to the most beautiful kitchen I have ever seen. Two ovens stacked on top of one another, an island straight off the TV with mini ceramic Christmas trees on either side, a refrigerator door designed to blend into the cabinets, and of course, there is one of those walk-in pantries bigger than my college dorm room. If only I could bake cookies in this place one day. If the little show between Shane and Stephanie is real, I will never come to this house again. *Closure sucks.*

I spot an old friend I lost contact with years ago sitting at the kitchen table with seating for at least twelve people, organizing the guests' Christmas cookies. Her genuine smile and confident wave excite me.

"Tara! Oh my God! How have you been? It's so good to see you!" Nadege calls out.

"It's awesome to see you too! I'm hanging in. Same old dose of stress every day." I walk over to the table.

"Tell me about it. I have two kids at home and a husband who is addicted to video games. Stress is my middle name. Are those what I think they are?" She points at the tins I'm hugging close to my body for dear life. They will not need rescuing again.

"Yes, indeed. Fresh out of the oven." I open the top tin and offer her one. She declines with a wave of her hand.

"I promised myself I wouldn't eat any cookies before the judging. I need to fit into my pants at least for a few good pictures first."

"Ha-ha." I miss how easy Nadege makes me laugh. My smile wilts when I notice a blue tin of spritz cookies with a small flag sticking up with the word, winner, written on it. They must be Shane's. He is fighting dirty tonight. I silently thank my mother for the heads up.

"Let me guess who made those cookies?" I glare at Shane's cookies. They look delicious. He used food coloring like I did and added a lot more sprinkles than me. Grr, the shapes he used are the same ones that got rusted the last time I made these cookies. I curse under my breath.

"If I remember correctly, your cookies were the best," she reminds me. Nadege hides the side of her mouth with the palm of her hand. "As the story goes, he cried in the boy's locker room after home economics and asked for a nurse's pass to get out of gym."

A laugh escapes my throat. "Nadege, I would love nothing more than to believe that, but he has always been too tough and proud ever to admit that to anyone."

"He told Stephanie that's what happened."

I never hated Stephanie in my life, even though she has always been friends with Shane. A flash of anger heats my blood and pounds through my head. She wasted no time sinking her manicured claws into the newly single Shane Brooks. If I wanted a chance, I'm already too late. They are already wearing matching sloth sweaters, my favorite animal. *I need a drink.*

"Lucky Stephanie. If Shane did cry, that's crazy. They are only cookies. Shane and I both got an A in the class anyway, and neither of us grew up to be master chefs. It didn't matter who won a silly high school challenge."

Nadege opens her mouth to speak, but a soft, tenor voice that once asked if he could kiss me interrupts her.

"Yes, it mattered. That class was always about us," Shane says from behind me. "I wanted there to be an us."

I turn toward his heartfelt words, ignoring the emotional whiplash. Shane is alone without Stephanie hanging all over him.

"Does Stephanie know that?" I ask before I can take it back.

A flicker of a side smile grazes his lips. "We're just old friends, helping each other through a hard time. Nothing more than commiseration."

"Oh, I remember that word from tenth grade! I definitely spelled it wrong on the SATs," Nadege interjects. I ignore her and surrender to the crimson flecks of Shane's gaze.

"I'm sorry things are rough. That's cool that Stephanie is helping. Take it one day at a time, Shane." I infuse some sincerity into my voice. I believe him, but this sinking ship is done. *Maybe this party will be about letting him go*? I understand caring for an old friend during a break-up, but her kiss on his cheek means this is something more whether he knows it or not.

Shane purses his lips into a flat line and nods. In an instant, his asshole smirk comes back. "I know what will lift my spirits. Would you like to try the winning cookie, Tara?" He fans out his hand as if he is presenting a prized yacht.

I glance back at the cookie table, purposely ignoring the left top corner where his tin sits. "Hmm, who will be the winner this year? Sugar cookies with royal icing, or the gingerbread men? Those peppermint meringues at the end of the table look yummy. I can't wait to try them all."

"Very funny, Tara. The Cookie Showdown starts at nine o'clock. I will be here guarding the winner. I wouldn't want anyone confusing mine with yours." He tilts his chin toward the tins I'm still clutching to my chest.

"There will be no confusion. It's all in the taste."

"We shall see, my dear. Looking good, by the way."

My heart and brain can't catch up fast enough. By the time a witty comeback pops into my mind, Shane has a fresh beer from the fridge and is walking out of the room, grinning against the curved opening of the bottle.

"What the hell was that cat and mouse game?" Nadege asks.

"This is not about cookies anymore. It's revenge."

Chapter Four

Out of all the other people's cookies, I eat ten, nibble a little bit off the rest, and leave Shane's cookie untouched. My favorite is the hot chocolate peppermint thumbprint cookies from a girl I barely remember. She stands in the corner like a deer in headlights watching everyone eat. She smiles when I walk over and praise her baking skills.

"It's an old family recipe," she explains. "I hope I didn't take too much of a chance with them."

"I love the combo of flavors. The taste is so different," I compliment.

"Thank you for your kind words. It's not like I'm going to win next to your cookies."

"Sometimes, the queen has to step down and let someone else wear the crown." I'm a philosophical drunk. My hangover will suck tomorrow, but Stephanie's homemade mulled wine makes me feel no pain. I chugged the first glass too fast after my run-in with Shane. I take another big gulp from my third glass catching his gaze again from across the kitchen. He has not let me out of his sight since the cookie tasting began. I refuse to lift his perfect green wreath spritz cookie to my mouth, and he knows it. He won't catch me eating his losing cookie.

The girl I still can't place in my memory touches my arm and moves on to the next ex-classmate. I'm alone, inspecting the sea of faces in the crowd. Everyone looks the same except for some thinning hairlines or big rocks on the girls' fingers. I wanted to be in this crowd years ago. They all seemed out of reach, except for Shane. He would have brought me inside this inner circle if the events of the past differed.

"You didn't try my cookie," Shane scolds. I gasp, and my mulled wine splashes onto my sweater. He sighs and shakes his head, peering down at my chest. "I told you to be more careful."

"Don't sneak up on people like that!" I wipe my hand on the definite wine stain. My best friend is going to kill me. "For your information, I'm saving the worst cookie for last." I flash him a sassy smile.

"Now, you're flirting with me. How many cups of wine did it take?"

"If this is your idea of flirting, what's your take on foreplay?" The words vomit out of my mouth. I look away and sip the remnants of my drink.

"Ah, I see. Adult Tara is a tease, or rather a drunk Tara likes to play." Shane inches close enough so I have to look up at him. I forgot how much shorter I am than him. I step back, hitting my lower back against the countertop. A lot of people crowd the kitchen, leaving nowhere else for me to go.

"First off, I am not drunk, just pleasantly buzzed. Secondly, I am not a tease. I was standing here minding my own business until you crashed into my party of one. You keep finding me."

"Well, damn. You figured me out, huh? Maybe I rushed over here after your mom texted my mom hoping I would get to see you."

My heart skips a beat but restarts. He's lying. There

is no way he made all those cookies less than two hours ago. I pick up his spritz cookie and take a bite into heaven. This is a perfect cookie. He must have baked them this morning. They taste fresh, with a hint of vanilla.

"Nice try, Shane. I'm flattered, but my mom only reached out an hour before the party. You couldn't have made these cookies right before you came."

"Like you did? Your cookie was still warm."

"I had to work today, so yes, I made them before I came. You figured out my big secret. Good for you." I tap my wine glass against his very white sweater. Shane looks down, frowning. My ugly sweater reindeer is almost kissing his Christmas sloth. There I go again. My thoughts heading for the gutter, full speed ahead.

"I'm still going to win," Shane reaffirms.

"Make up your mind, Shane. Either be the funny, sweet guy from high school or stick with being a jerk. I can't keep up with your mood swings."

Shane cocks his head to the side, all his softness and confusing remarks gone.

"I can see where I'm not wanted. Sorry, Tara," he says. He steps away from me, backing up into the crowd.

I gasp, and my hand shoots out, grabbing Shane's hard bicep. He smiles as he peeks over his shoulder.

Before another wisecrack falls from his mouth, Stephanie calls for attention in the room. One of the old Football players makes a loud whistle with his fingers in his mouth, silencing the commotion in the kitchen.

"Thank you. I'm so happy everyone came to my mini-reunion, and holy crap, these cookies are amazing. Tonight has been the best! We are going to start the judging for our contest in a few minutes. Melissa will pass out the scorecards soon. There is only one rule. Do not vote for yourself. Make someone else happy tonight. Let's get started!" Stephanie claps, and everyone else does too, except for me because I'm still holding onto Shane's arm.

"Ahem, if I'm going to win this competition, I will need my arm back." Shane winks down at me.

I release him. There he goes switching back to an asshole. Someone cranks the music back up louder than before.

"Your cookie is good, but I'm pretty certain I'm still going to win," I shout.

"Want to bet?" Shane crosses his arms over his chest. He licks his upper lip, drawing my gaze to his pouty mouth. His lips have always been full and naturally soft. I could ask for a kiss if I win. One last chance and woo him away from Stephanie. I shake my head back and forth, banishing the wine-fueled craziness.

"I only have twenty dollars in my wallet. With our history, that isn't much of a wager. I'll pass," I force out of my mouth through gritted teeth.

"I wasn't interested in a money bet." He grazes his thumb over my cheek close to my mouth. His finger comes away with a smudge of chocolate and heads straight into his mouth. Shane sucks the stray chocolate off his finger, moaning while staring at me. *God, that was hot.*

"I am not covering my body with chocolate syrup so you can lick it off me. That is my one rule." I roll my eyes. I keep bringing the conversation back to sex. I must remember Stephanie hanging all over him earlier in the night.

Shane's eyes widen, and he laughs. "You said it, not me. I am fine with that rule. I want something simpler."

His gaze wanders my body, and I wonder if he is pondering the chocolate option I threw out there.

"What do you want if you win?" I ask. I take another big sip of my wine.

"A date."

I almost spit my wine back into the stem glass. *Did Shane just ask me out on a date?* I fail miserably at concealing my disbelief, coughing up the rest of the wine lingering in my throat. To my horror, Shane pats my back.

"A date? You barely know me anymore. How could you want to go out with me after the sucker punches we keep taking at each other?"

Melissa, the gossip queen, chooses this moment to hand out the scorecards. Shane wrinkles his nose and sticks his tongue out at her as she squeezes through the small space between us. When she is out of earshot, Shane says, "Maybe I'm a glutton for punishment or I regret how we left things in high school."

Without delving too deep into his words, I ask, "What do I get if I win?"

"Let's figure it out if that happens." Another wink from him threatens my willpower. I'm a goner for the mischievous glint in his eyes when he's being playful. It was my downfall when he asked me to the football game that night he kissed me.

"You're so sure of yourself."

Shane leans in toward my ear and places both of his hands on the countertop behind me, effectively caging me in. His breath tickles the side of my neck, and his lips graze my ear. "Yup, and before this night is through, I will suck more chocolate off your skin."

His warm breath sends shivers down my arm. My hand feels up his chest resting on the face of the sloth. Shane moves my hand off his body. "Only if I win. Do you accept?"

The cocky hot guy is never easy. There is always a catch. "Yes."

"All right, Ms. Spritz Cookie Champion. The showdown is on. See you on the other side."

Shane takes his pen and marks a big x next to his name. *He is already cheating in order to win, um, me?*

Something is not right. My bullshit radar stands at full alert, sobering me up to square one. I must find out what is going on, and I know just the person to tell me.

Chapter Five

I wait until Melissa hands everyone the scorecards, and then I pounce. My gaze lingers on a few of them in my periphery, catching glimpses of my name circled on the top. Whoever made these cards is aware of the strife between Shane and me. My name is at the top, and Shane's name is at the bottom. All the other cookie messes are between us.

Melissa sits down at the kitchen table with her box of cookies and nibbles on each one. Her favorite also seems to be the hot chocolate peppermint thumbprint cookies I like because she finishes the entire cookie and draws a star next to the girl's name. *Yes, Lisa is her name!*

I inhale a deep breath. "Hey, Melissa, do you have a second to talk?"

"Are you going to say yes to the date with Shane?" Melissa hollers over the loud music. She grins and peers up at me.

I knew she scooted between him and me on purpose! Damn, she must have some killer sharp hearing. Shane's voice drops a few octaves whenever he wants something. This time it is a real date with me.

"My God, not so loud. I agreed, but there are conditions to it."

"He's been asking me about you for weeks. What conditions could that idiot be talking about, now?"

A bead of sweat rolls down my forehead. "I see you all the time in the supermarket, and you talk about everything under the sun, except for that information? Melissa, I'm so in the dark right now. What do you know about Shane?"

Like a classic snitch, she searches the kitchen for him. He should be downstairs in the finished basement with some of the football team. Stephanie followed him down, too, shutting the door behind her.

"He asked Stephanie to invite you to the party, and I made sure it happened."

"Yeah, so his cookies can win, and I would be miserable in my defeat, right?" I fold my hands over my chest, taping my boot on the linoleum floor. My irritation peaks as I glance back at the closed basement door.

After eating a pretzel cookie with candy melted on top, Melissa shakes her head up and down. "I'm dead serious. This was all planned to get you here, so he could see you again and maybe ask you out. Give the man a chance. He had his heart ripped out of his chest by his ex. He's bruised all over."

My broken heart thumps in my chest. The kitchen is hot as hell, but my emotions are boiling up to the surface. After all this time, Shane wants another chance.

"What happened to him?" I ask.

"Well, he proposed to his girlfriend, and she said no. She moved out of their apartment the next morning. New York City rents suck, so he came home when his lease was up a month ago. His ex will not speak to him. Stephanie checked her social media, and she already has someone new. Break-ups in your twenties can be harsh, but this hurt him. Stephanie and her boyfriend Brian have been hanging out a lot with Shane to cheer him up. All your jealousy at Stephanie and Shane is wasted energy."

I'm thankful I still have cookies left. I pick up the gingerbread man and bite off his head. At least Shane's ex had the decency to say no at the proposal and not down the aisle. Poor guy, but after his relationship fiasco, I'm the one who is on his mind? I have only seen him a few times in the past ten years, and only one of those times we spoke about the least interesting thing in the world. The weather, of course. *He cannot be still holding the torch for me.*

"You don't believe me. I know my fair share of gossip, but these are facts, Tara. He likes you and wants that date," Melissa confirms. She touches my hand.

"What about the scene between Stephanie and Shane when I showed up? Can she be more territorial?"

Melissa scoffs. "She's always like that with everyone. Honestly, nothing is going on between them."

Ugh, I love having trust issues on top of everything else. I glance behind Melissa at the photo tiles lining the walls. Stephanie is draped over the same guy in three of the photos. This must be the boyfriend.

"I want this to be real. I would love to go out with him and find out who he is as an adult. He gave me my first kiss. I hope he gives me my next." I blurt out the truth. Melissa fake fans herself with a chocolate chip cookie, pretending to be choked up. "All right, you can say it."

"Aww, maybe it will happen. Have a little Christmas hope. By the way, you look fabulous tonight. I love that you still curl your hair at the ends. Your sweater is hilarious too."

"I wish I were wearing a cocktail dress. Who picked this theme anyway?" I pick at my scratchy neckline.

"I did," Melissa admits.

"Well, it was an adorable idea and a great ice breaker for the awkwardness of the party."

Melissa's smile returns, picking up on my attempt to climb out of the hole. "I know it's silly, but everyone is always so busy and glum during the holidays when they come home. I get it. No one wants to leave their perfect lives and peek back on the past. If we all smile and bake cookies more, maybe Christmas won't be so bad after all."

"You made me very happy aside from the whole Shane thing. I hadn't baked spritz cookies since my last boyfriend broke up with me. I liked having a positive reason for baking them."

"And who knows? You might possibly get a date or kick Shane's ass if you win. All great reasons for baking cookies." She finds my cookie and takes a bite. "His ass is officially beaten. Wow, these are good."

"Thank you. I have to figure out what I want from him if I win. I'm all confused now."

"Tell him to spill his guts about following you around the mall a few weeks ago."

I cock my head to one side. "The mall? I hardly ever go there." *There's more to Shane's obsession with me?*

"You did recently, and he spotted you. He said your hair was straightened, and you were wearing a dress."

Shane must have seen me after I got my hair blown out for an engagement party. I ran around the mall like a crazy woman looking for matching shoes for this awful dress my mother gave me. Figures that would be the day he saw me.

"Yes, I know when you're talking about. He followed me?"

"For about twenty minutes. He wasn't sure it was you, but you stared right at him without realizing it. He thought you looked so pretty. Even without wearing a dress tonight, you are making him drool."

I probably did see him but missed him because I was lost in my own thoughts.

"Can you keep this between us? Please, don't tell him I told you any of this stuff," Melissa whispers. She bites into some Christmas bark, wincing.

"I promise I won't say anything. I will let him fawn over me all by himself. Are you okay?"

She grabs her water bottle and chugs almost half of it. "That Christmas crack has way too much sugar in it. I think I'm done eating cookies. You got my vote."

"Thank you for voting for me and letting me know about Shane."

"You're welcome." Melissa checks the timer on the oven. "Voting time is almost up. I need to collect the cards. Good luck, Tara; I'm rooting for you." She gets up and starts asking people if they completed the cards.

I'm left alone at the table of cookies, temptation daring me into stealing a broken gingerbread man. Shane appears, scooting onto the chair next to me, bumping his arm into mine.

"Ouch!" I tease him. "Are you trying to take out your opponent?" I try hiding my smile. He smiles, too, pretending everything Melissa told me is not on his shoulders right now.

"Interesting choice of words, Tara. Yes, I'm trying to take you out, but only if I win. If you win, I'll shovel the snow off your parents' driveway all winter."

"Excuse me. No deal. My dad has a snowblower, and it barely snowed last year. I want something better."

"How about I let you know my secret for my special spritz cookies?"

"Weak, but I'll bite. Add in a kiss under the mistletoe, and you have a deal."

Apparently, I can successfully flirt without his arms almost around me and his breath not against my neck. Shane slowly turns my way, and his side smile while glancing down at my lips, knocks sexy right out of the park. If there was not a cookie challenge to win, I would leave with him right now if he wants me this bad.

A low chuckle glides from his mouth. "Deal. You were sitting a long time with Melissa. Do I have to talk to her about oversharing?"

I lean my face as close to him as I can without our lips touching. His cocksure smile returns. "I haven't the slightest idea what you're talking about, Shane. Excuse me while I get a good seat for the winning announcements. Good luck!" I purse my lips and kiss the air between us. I smile as his lips pucker, expecting more.

"Same to you, teasing Tara."

I flip him the middle finger as I rise out of my chair. I grab a new plastic cup and pour myself a generous helping of the mulled wine. I'm proud of my newfound courage, however long it lasts.

The announcements will be held in the huge living room outside of the kitchen. As I make my way through the swinging door, Shane watches my every move. I peek back at him, and bingo, there he is waving my way.

If either of us wins, this outcome will be quite interesting.

Chapter Six

The music cuts out, and our hostess steps up on her parents' coffee table with the help of Shane. Stephanie mouths *thank you* to Shane, and the urge to separate them nudges me. My jealousy flares up, but I take a deep breath remembering Melissa's words. All of this is a setup. Shane sits down on the couch opposite where I'm standing, making us in perfect view of each other. He stares up at Stephanie as if he is an innocent bystander.

Damn jerk is going to win.

"Ladies and drunk jocks, we have our winners! Before I announce them, please give a round of applause for the cookie bakers and those who had to take their belts off because they ate too many!" Stephanie shouts.

Everyone claps, and some guy whips his belt around his head like a lasso. The applause dies down, and Melissa hands Stephanie a folded piece of paper and three red envelopes.

"Give it up one more time for Melissa! The cookie baking contest was her idea." People clap again, and Melissa takes a small bow.

"Behold our winners." Stephanie unfolds the piece of paper, raising her eyebrows in surprise. "Third place goes to Dennis for his White Chocolate Christmas Bark patties! Here is a gift certificate to the Old Village inn, donated by yours truly."

Dennis, one of the only guys who has lost his hair,

steps up to Stephanie, and she kisses him on the cheek. The pack of jocks all cheer for their homeboy as he returns to their corner.

"And second place goes to Nadege for her Lemon Ricotta cookies. They were my personal favorite. Please leave the rest of them before you go. You will receive a free massage at the Exclusive Day Spa, donated by Melissa's parents."

Nadege finds her way through the crowded room up to Stephanie. "I'll make them any time you want. I'm so excited to go to the spa."

Melissa adds, "Tell them you're friends with the owner's daughter, and they will fix you up nicely."

"Thank you, ladies!" Nadege smiles, accepting her prize.

The couch springs creek as a certain someone stands up prematurely for his reward. Shane rubs his hands together in front of his face, warming up for his victory. He brushes sweater lint off the sloth's face and stares up at Stephanie.

"And now, what we all have been waiting for. Drum roll, please."

The jocks bang on any surface available, louder each second, and some people howl into their cupped hands. Any second now, I will lose to Shane Brooks, and he will have his date. A rush of relief relaxes my shoulders and slips a smile onto my face. I almost skipped this party. Another year I will get my revenge for Shane's rigged cookie contest stunt.

"The first prize of a hundred-dollar gift certificate to Wyatt's Steak House goes to Lisa Fitzpatrick and her delicious hot chocolate peppermint thumbprint cookies! Thank you, everyone, again for baking! Same time next year!"

A "What" slides right out of my mouth. All eyes are on me, but my gaze is on Shane, snatching the piece of paper with Lisa's name written on it. Stephanie reaches for his hand to step off the coffee table, but he ignores her and re-reads the winners' names over and over.

"I thought I was supposed to win?" Shane whispers to Stephanie. Her gaze shifts to me and back to Shane. I already believe Melissa's story about how I wound up at this party, but Stephanie's actions just proved it.

She steps down off the coffee table by herself and pats Shane on the chest, "Some of this had to be done on your own. If it makes you feel any better, there was basically a three-way tie between you, Tara, and Lisa. We took another vote while you and Tara were flirting like school kids at the table, and Lisa came out on top."

Stephanie hands Lisa her gift certificate. "You won fair and square. Your cookies were the best."

"I can't believe it. Thank you so much. Tara, I hope you're not mad at me?" Lisa asks.

I hear her, but my gaze is on Shane. Disappointment stains his face with a red flush to his cheeks. He lost twice now, and neither of us won.

Is the bet still on?

Lisa touches my arm, and I finally turn toward her. "I'm not mad at all. Remember what I said in the kitchen? Sometimes the queen bee needs to step down. Your cookies were good. Enjoy the restaurant. The new chef is amazing." I smile at Lisa, and I mean every word.

"Yummy. I'm so excited. If you ever want the thumbprint recipe, let me know," Lisa offers.

I nod and notice Shane is no longer standing off to the side of the coffee table. I search around me, but he's gone. Shane towers over most of the people in this room. *Ugh, I stop staring at him for one second, and he just bails?*

"Where did Shane go?" I ask Stephanie.

"Uh, he was right here a second ago. I have his keys, so he can't go far."

A loud crash echoes from the kitchen. A male voice yells, and multiple female giggles follow. I run to the swinging door, shouting Shane's name at the top of my lungs.

"*Shane!*"

Chapter Seven

"Wait, don't come any closer!" Shane calls out before I register the scene.

His once white sweater, with the cute sloth, has red wine all over it, and two girls sit on the floor in a large puddle. One of them laughs so hard, she slips onto her back. Two plastic cups rest next to them, and the shattered glass from the crockpot lid lays on the floor between them.

"There is glass everywhere. Go get Stephanie and Melissa, Tara. I don't want you slipping," Shane instructs.

"We slipped!" The girls cackle. The one on her back spreads her arms out, making an angel in the spilled wine. "Ouch, this glass hurts!"

Shane and I gawk at the messy girls, and memories of them being sloppy at every school dance pop into my head. Tiffany and Charlotte always together, wasted or high. They thought it was so cool sneaking vodka into their water bottles. Now, they are just annoying. Shane sighs and tugs off the soaked sweater over his head.

Both girls and I stop and stare at his exposed arms and the part of his chest left uncovered by his undershirt.

"Hubba, hubba, welcome to the gun show, Shane," Tiffany woos. She flexes her non-muscular arms.

"I think I'm going to stay right here. This is the best view in the house!" Charlotte remarks. She lies down on her back in the wine and glass.

I'm still standing just inside the doorjamb, drool pooling in my mouth. The sneak peek of Shane's body stops me from getting whomever for help.

"Oh, Tara? Remember me? The loser who ruined Stephanie's sweater a few minutes ago. I'm wet and sticky." Shane waves his hand in my direction.

I open and close my mouth, settling for a simple nod. Shane rolls his eyes and covers his chest with his sweater. I spot his signature sly side smile. *Someone likes the attention…*

"Here, distraction gone," Shane says. He tilts his head to the side. "Go on, now."

I nod again and walk backward into the living room, not letting Shane out of my sight until the door swings back. Everyone else gathers around the huge Christmas tree selecting small pieces of paper out of a large red bucket. My focus has been solely on the cookies, so I forgot about the ten-dollar gift exchange.

Melissa separates from the pack, aiming for me.

"Is Shane okay? He wanted to win so bad!"

Away from his incredible body, I have a voice again. "Yeah. One of the Trouble Twins knocked over the crockpot. The lid broke too. We need a mop."

"I know I volunteered as the party mom, but seriously? Those girls are cut off. I'll be back," Melissa scoffs. "Watch those harlots. They need to keep their paws off your man."

I laugh before I realize she's right. I go back into the kitchen, and Shane, the convenient gentleman, helps Charlotte off the floor. The muscles in his back ripple with his movements. I quietly thank every gym he has ever been to for his hot physique. Charlotte walks carefully to the cookie table, and Shane helps Tiffany up as well. His gaze meets mine. He mouths, *Save me.*

"Every fireman needs a body like Shane. I would burn my house down for some mouth to mouth." Tiffany leans into Shane, smacking her lips together.

"All right, ladies break it up," I say. I clap my hands. "Shane is a human being, not a piece of meat."

"You talk so sweetly to me. Is anyone coming with a mop?" Shane asks. He rings out his poor ugly sweater into the sink.

"Yup, Melissa. Do you have any other clothes?"

"Yeah, I planned on staying over. I have clothes upstairs. Be right back."

He brushes past me, heading into the hallway leading to the grand staircase by the front door. Ugh, he left me alone again. The drunk girls demolishing the leftover cookies don't count.

"Shane, wait!"

I follow him down the hallway. He stops and turns around at the foot of the entryway staircase. "I really want to get dry, Tara. Wait down here."

"But, what about our bet? The date, the kiss?"

His softer side appears for a moment. He brushes back my curls over my shoulder, leaning toward my right ear.

"We both lost, Tara. I was supposed to only get the date if I win. I guess the vanilla extract I used was expired," he whispers.

I have seconds for my move. Mistletoe hangs from the ceiling almost right above us, and bravery from out of nowhere grips hold of me. *This is it, my chance.*

As Shane pulls back from me, I caress the side of his face and turn his chin toward me. Our lips meet in the middle for the first kiss of hopefully many more. He tastes like sugar cookies and wine, churning together and never fading out. His hands find my hips, and mine wrap around his neck. A sigh of relief gets trapped between us.

We made it.

I step onto my tiptoes, hoping Shane takes more from me. My mouth, my heart, and my very soul. He can have everything.

Cold air from the front door pauses my paradise. Shane's mouth pulls away, and I open my eyes, dreading our stolen moment is over. His tongue darts out, licking his top lip with a smile.

"Sorry, my ride is here. I didn't mean to interrupt. Later, guys," an old classmate says. He waves as he sneaks out of the party.

Shane shivers, holding me close to the front of his body a second longer. He removes his hands from my waist and jerks his head toward the stairs.

"Come with me." *You never have to ask me twice…*

Chapter Eight

Stephanie's bathroom is practically the size of my last apartment. The room has a claw-footed tub, a double-long vanity, a fainting couch, and a shower with a separate closed alcove for the toilet. Shane locks the door and rests his head against the fluffy towels hanging there. We are officially alone. The only reminder of the party downstairs is the distant thump of the music.

"I'm sure we'll laugh about all of this tomorrow," Shane says. He strips out of his stained undershirt.

I sit down on the velvet couch in the middle of the room, watching him wet a hand towel and pat the residue wine off his chest. The ceiling-high vanity mirror confirms I am, in fact, salivating at the sight of him. My lips are also stained from the red wine. I quickly rub the inside of my sweater over my mouth before Shane catches my gaze in the mirror.

"I'm having a great time. I made my favorite Christmas cookie, listened to the latest gossip of the popular kids' grown-up style, watched drunk people make complete fools of themselves, and the best part was seeing you again." Shane flexes his arms, wiping them down. "On second thought, the best part is watching you clean up right now. You work out, huh?"

"After every break-up, I try to find myself again. A sad lie I keep telling myself. My last one was rough. I might have overdone it on the deadlifts," Shane remarks.

He leans his back against the counter, staring at me.

Back in high school, I swooned over Shane's sincerity and ability to show me his real self. His rejection hurt more because of it. Young love never lasts, but it always stings if the memory curls up at the wrong moment.

"I understand that lie all too well." Biting the inside of my cheek, I hope what I ask doesn't sabotage whatever this can be for Shane and me, but I must know. "Why did you get so mad when you lost the cookie test in the eleventh grade? We had kissed the day before, and then you took it away."

His eyes widen, and his lips form a harsh line. He ruffles a hand through his hair, releasing a long breath. "Will the old 'It wasn't you; it was me' excuse work?"

"You have to explain part of it then. I'll take anything," I plead.

"Remember my next-door neighbor, Nick Davies?"

"Of course, I do. I went to junior prom with him. We dated until the beginning of summer, and then he dumped me. Didn't you two have a big falling out?"

"Yup, because of you."

The last thing I want to do tonight at the start of my sugar crash is regret one of my first serious relationships. "You're blaming me, now?"

Topless Shane saunters over to the fainting couch. I scoot to the right side so he can sit down, but he has other plans. He gets down on one knee and drapes his hands over mine in my lap. His heat warms and calms me. He does affect me more than I want to admit.

"I'm the one to blame. I told Nick I kissed you, and he freaked out. He told me how he always liked you and wanted to ask you to prom. I got cold feet. I caved and told him I would step aside if you won the cookie contest in home economics. Of course, your cookies won. Tara, you have patience like no other. I rushed my batch, the bottoms got burnt, and they stuck to the pan because I was so nervous, I forgot to grease the cookie sheet. I was upset because I liked you even though you were not in my crew. I dreamed of being with you, but then you won. I regretted my decision to let Nick ask you out for a long time. I brushed it off as raging hormones. Then every time I came home after high school, you were always there wherever I went, but you never saw me. I thought it was the universe telling me something, but I ignored it until now. I like you, and maybe we could be something now?"

I inwardly sigh at his confession. If you told me earlier, I would be sitting here with Shane Brook's naked chest staring at me while he reveals eleven-year-old secrets, I would've laughed and asked for more wine. I want to say yes to the man of my teenage dreams before I think about it too much.

"If I put a shirt on, will you pretend that you heard me talking?"

I giggle and close the space between our lips. His kiss feels even better without any wager hindering my feelings or high school politics keeping us apart. He lets me drag him up from his knees. I lean back onto the arm of the couch, and Shane drapes his body over mine.

"Does this mean you forgive me?" Shane asks.

"Yes, just lay off the betting for a while, okay?"

Shane nods and crushes his lips against mine.

Would it be bad if we fooled around now? We should go on a date first, right?

The inviting hardness of his body grinding into my

pelvis tempts me into going further, snatching my ugly sweater over my head. My move separates us, both of us whimpering at the loss.

Shane's gaze roams over my green tank top. My breasts are thrust up in a lacey push-up bra, slightly exposed.

"Merry Christmas." Shane moans and kisses my collarbone before working his way down to the tops of my breasts. His mouth feels timeless like this is the next day of our relationship.

Shane never left my thoughts over the years. I replayed the memory of my first kiss countless times. My other boyfriends' kisses never quite measured up.

"Shane, are we really going to do it in Stephanie Myerson's bathroom?" I ask. Shane's delectable mouth kisses further beneath my bra.

He freezes over me. "Good point. What was I thinking giving you up?" Shane reluctantly adjusts my tank top over my breasts. He gives them one last caress before lifting off me.

"I thought you hated me," I admit. I pick up my sweater from the bathroom floor.

"Never. But, when you won history day, I might have disliked you for about a week."

"I won fair and square!"

"Blah, blah, blah. I found original newspaper articles from over a hundred years ago, and all I got was a participation ribbon."

I shrug. "All right, I guess I'll just go home and think about what I did eleven years ago."

Shane curls his arm around my bare shoulders. "Don't you dare. Apart from our wager, I promised to lick chocolate off a part of your body before the night ends. I take my promises very seriously."

A knock at the door interrupts the temptation of throwing morality aside and making out with him in Stephanie's claw-footed tub.

"Are you lovebirds finished yet? Other people have to pee, you know!"

I don't recognize the shouting male voice, but he halts my naughty mind. Shane flips his middle finger at the door. He kisses me one more time before I stand up.

"Come on, show me where we are staying tonight?"

Shane's sly grin emerges. "Follow me."

Chapter Nine

The line outside of the upstairs bathroom stretches about ten people long, wrapped down the hallway. Everyone with screaming bladders shoots daggers at us. They all start clapping as I hide behind Shane's back.

"I thought the walk of shame was supposed to be the morning after?" I mumble. Embarrassment overcomes me, and I tug my sweater back on.

"There are five other bathrooms in this mansion, and all of you have to use this one?" Shane yells.

I peek at the line of people. The first guy hurries past us into the bathroom, slamming the door shut. The others gasp, seeing me with Shane. *I guess I am not the only one who mistakenly thought Shane and Stephanie were together.*

"All right, break it up, people. Upstairs is off-limits. No more hanky panky in the champagne room, except for these two," Stephanie explains from behind us. She is wearing a different outfit, and her hair is up in a ponytail. Some of her makeup is gone, and she is carrying a wine glass in each hand.

Her boyfriend, the guy in the picture downstairs, opens the door behind her. "Coast clear?"

I don't see much of him, but Stephanie's loud sigh tells me either they just fooled around or were about to.

"No. Stay inside, please." She shoos him back into the bedroom. He shuts the door. "If I'm not getting laid at my own party with my boyfriend, no one is getting some. Please go downstairs so the magic can happen." Her smile is fierce, just like high school.

The nine people waiting in line take the hint and hurry down the stairs. I'm stuck beside Shane, unsure what to do next.

"As you were," Stephanie remarks. She salutes us with the empty wine glass stained with lipstick on the side.

The guy who got into the bathroom comes out whistling, avoiding all our faces, and sprints down the stairs. When he is out of sight, Shane thanks Stephanie and grabs my hand, pulling me toward the other end of the hall.

The guest room with Shane's suitcase laying on the bed is just as big as the kitchen. The bed itself must be bigger than a king. "Wow," I gasp.

"Still admiring the view?" Shane asks. He opens his suitcase and grabs a fresh undershirt.

"Multiple views. This bed is ridiculous."

"You have no idea. Lie down. I swear I won't try any funny business until you marinate in the softness. That bed can wish the day away."

For a moment, I forget the room, the bed, and since Shane has a shirt on, I can think again. He sounds like he used to back in high school. Funny, sweet, and a gentleman. The switch has taken place. Shane Brooks is all mine, and I'm not letting go.

"Go on. Try it out," Shane insists.

I take off my boots, praying my feet don't smell. I climb up onto the large bed and crawl toward the multiple sets of throw pillows. I lie back on them, basking in the comfortable euphoria settling over me.

Shane completes this dream by laying on his side and caressing my stomach underneath my sweater.

"Isn't this bed heaven on earth?"

"You are heaven on earth." I shut my eyes. *Did I just say that?*

Without a pause, he says, "You haven't even had the best part." He reaches behind him, grabbing a small cookie box off the nightstand. "We can just lie here, eat cookies, and if you take off your ugly sweater, the real fun will begin."

Shane kisses me slow this time, learning how perfectly our lips curve together. His warm hand cups the side of my face. Without losing contact, we scoot closer, crunching the cookie box between us. The big bed makes me wonder how many times we can roll around making love and not fall off. I smile against Shane's lip, interrupting his French kisses.

"Happy, Tara?" Shane smiles now too.

"So happy. Let's not smush the cookies any further. We'll eat them after."

"Okay. Lose your sweater too. You can wear it after."

I laugh and remove my friend's sweater as Shane shoves the cookies back on the nightstand. We move to the center of the bed, and Shane rolls me on top of him, straddling his lap. "Kiss me again."

I reply with a grind of my hips and a whisper of yes against his lips.

The first time we make love, we roll three and a half times without falling off the bed. The second time, four complete rolls with me back on top, hoping I can lie on Shane's chest, breathing in the mixture of strong cologne and the lingering aroma of stale wine forever.

Chapter Ten

One year later

"Promise me you won't get mad," Shane asks.

"What did you do?"

"I dropped one." Shane lowers his head until his chin hits his neck.

I know what this means…

My mom's counter is at a hundred and fifteen days without our dog stealing stuff from the floor. I point at the sign, and Shane flips the numbers back to zero. Mickey's heavy breathing and lopsided smile from underneath the kitchen table drives away any remorse.

"I hope it was one of yours."

"Yup, no worries. Your perfect spritz cookies are still all intact, except for the three I ate already."

"Shane!" I shout. I grab my cookie tins and move them over to the kitchen table, away from his sticky fingers. Shane follows close behind me. His magical hands wrap around my waist, and he squeezes me back into him. I love his arms around me; there is no other place I feel this good.

My boyfriend, Shane Brooks, nuzzles his lips against my neck. *If only there was time to play.*

"Your kisses ruin me. We are going to cut it close for everything tonight. Before dinner at your parents' house, we still need to stop by the apartment, and after all of that, Stephanie's party starts at eight."

"We can be late to all of the above." One hand, still warm from taking cookies out of the oven moments before, makes its way up my shirt, caressing upward.

"You call your mother and tell her exactly why we're going to be late," I say.

Shane stops his sneaky quest. He kisses my cheek from behind and moves away from me.

"We will have enough time for a quick make-out session in our new kitchen. We have to break it in and christen all surfaces." Shane shifts more hot cookies onto the drying rack.

"The contractor barely started yet. They only put in the new cabinets. Hopefully, his team finishes before the new year. Fingers crossed."

"I can't wait. At least your parents went to the mountains for the holidays. I love you, but your mother's questions are a little much."

"She means well. I remember she made me so nervous about possibly seeing you again before Stephanie's party last year."

"I was already at Stephanie's house when your mom texted my mom. I sat on the bottom of the stairs waiting for you."

"If I remember correctly, you told me you whipped up your cookies in the shortest amount of time imaginable and then rushed over to get revenge on me."

Shane steals another cookie and brings it up to his delectable mouth. "I lied." He bites into a red wreath spritz cookie with green sprinkles on top. He moans, and I regret stopping his wandering hands before. It has been almost two weeks since we have been staying at my parents' house. I miss being alone in our apartment. Six months of living together with epic TV show binges, dinner parties, board games, and uninterrupted sex.

Shane is hottest when he is cooking with or without clothes. Sometimes, he adds an apron for comedic effect. I can never resist a man who kneads cookie dough the way he does at least once a week. I will miss our old kitchen, but Shane will have to bake cookies in a brand-new kitchen with clothing optional.

The landlord promised us he would finish upgrading the appliances, the countertops, the cabinets, and refinish the floors. These repairs are a long time coming and inconveniently getting done around the holidays. The smell and the noise of repairs left us no choice but to stay at my parents' house for a few weeks.

At least, Shane has held up surprisingly well. My mom only asked him about our future wedding fifty times, give or take. I love him more each day for making up some appeasing bullshit for her. I keep reminding her, I'm not engaged yet, and she just smiles and points to her watch. Our apartment needs to be finished now.

Shane finishes a text message and slams down his phone with a huge grin on his face.

"What?"

Shane scoops me up into his arms as I yelp. "I just bought us another half hour alone."

"You're ridiculous."

"You love me."

"I love you with all my heart." I kiss the love of my life again and again.

****

We hike our way up the long path leading to Stephanie Myerson's front door. Shane holds my hand and has the bag with our cookies in it draped over his shoulder.

There isn't a lot of people here this year, only a chosen few. The gossip queen, Melissa, answers the door before I can knock.

"Hi! I'm so excited you came! Both of you!" She moves away from the door so we can enter.

"Hey, Melissa. Merry Christmas!"

"You too! Did you bring them?" Melissa peers behind Shane. He swings the Christmas tote bag off his shoulder and hands them over to her.

"Of course, we brought the winning cookies! We learned our lesson last time. I also brought a change of clothes just in case the twins are invited again," Shane jokes.

"Ha-ha, you're going to give everyone a run for their money."

"We plan on it," both Shane and I say in unison.

Melissa smiles and lifts a polaroid camera. "Say cheese, cuties."

Shane and I lean in and smile for the picture. Melissa hands it to us after the small film pops out of the top.

"We should put that on our new refrigerator."

"Great idea." The development of the pic is fast. Within minutes, Shane and my smiling faces stare back at us. We look happy. I feel happy.

"Are you ready to win the cookie showdown this year, babe?" Shane reaches his hand out to me.

"Absolutely."

Candy Cane Cookie Cover-Up

by

Jael Allen

Christmas Cookies Series

Dedication

To Cousin Sheila, my cookie dealer—
thank you for everything, especially my sugar fix!

Nick Morgan walked the three blocks from his hotel to Club Brizo in San Diego on a warm Friday night in October, not as a patron, but with an eye to adding the site to his upscale nightclub chain. Peyton Stewart, his best friend, right-hand man, and CEO, had whittled down their top southern California prospects to Brizo. If their efforts were successful, San Diego would become the third city to join Las Vegas and Seattle in Nick's growing enterprise. This trip would determine the final seal of approval before he and Peyton moved to the offer phase.

Nick entered the club, confirmed his reservation for the evening entertainment, and headed to the bar. Brizo's décor was black and silver with a long, L-shaped mahogany bar and high-backed, padded stools. The dining area boasted cushioned wooden seats as well, with round tables covered in pressed black linen and silver flickering candles. With less than thirty minutes before the show, well-dressed customers nursed drinks or ate from plates overflowing with tasty-looking morsels.

Nick claimed an empty stool at the center of the polished counter, ordered a dirty martini, and picked up the menu. Twenty minutes into his visit, the club had racked up points for quality, service, and ambiance and was at capacity. Lucy, one of two bartenders, checked to see if his drink needed to be replenished just as the stage lights began to dim. Nick declined her offer, swiveled his seat, and prepared to enjoy the show.

Thick curtains on the small, raised stage located behind the parquet dance square parted on the soft glow of a solitary beam to unveil the propped lid and back section of a baby grand piano. The room immediately quieted.

Moments later, a smooth male voice pierced the stillness. "Ladies and gentlemen, I give you…Siren!"

The room erupted with applause as the spotlight panned out to display a pair of killer stilettos, long, shapely legs, and the smooth skin of a well-toned thigh—all exposed by the generous slit of a shimmery, emerald gown. Seductive notes floated from the keys as the illumination expanded to reveal the three-quarter profile of a woman seated at the bench and thick, midnight-colored hair worked into an intricate knot at the base of her long, slender neck. Nick's gaze moved on to the creamy skin of her face…and his composure disintegrated.

He was going to kick Peyton's ass.

Also known as Ava Abbott—his runaway fiancée—Siren bowed her head, parted her glistening lips, and exhaled her first melody. Disbelief gripped Nick's mind, increased his heart rate, and hampered his ability to breathe. He absorbed the husky voice as it enveloped the crowd, and the familiar stab of long-buried pain sliced through his gut. Instinct urged him to leave, but his legs wouldn't obey. Instead, his gaze fixed on the image that had haunted his dreams for years, and—once again—he fell prey to the sound of her voice.

Though her gaze stayed glued to the keys, her throaty ballads and sultry serenades painted a poignant picture of life and loss. Erotic as the brush of a lover's fingers, her rich contralto teased his ears even as her words reached inside and squeezed his heart. Time passed unmarked until the last, traditional piece of her set. An aria with hints of Ireland and troubled seas, it vibrated through his body on shards of electric energy that continued to pulse even in the reverent hush that followed.

Only when the curtains began to close did cheers and applause erupt and the audience surge to their feet. Ava stood, gracefully stepped around her bench, and curtsied. Tonight she held her fans in the palm of her delicate hand, much as she had when he walked into Fusion, the small, hole-in-the-wall jazz club off the Vegas strip, where he'd first seen her perform.

That first night, after her performance, he'd waited for her in the main area—only to be told it was her routine to change and leave the building following her act. So Nick entrusted his card to Fusion's bartender with a generous tip and waited a week, but she didn't contact him. Undeterred, he returned twice more—leaving his card and a message each time—before she responded to his request.

As an agent, he'd been disappointed when Ava turned down his pitch to represent her. As a man, he'd been elated. In addition to her seductive singing persona, Ava had a blade-sharp wit and wicked sense of humor. She was also fiercely driven to ensure her harsh start in life would not define who she became.

Although she declined a business affiliation, their personal relationship blossomed over the ensuing months. He was so enthralled with her he proposed barely a year later on Christmas morning. That was the last time he'd seen her.

Until tonight.

This time, when the drapes closed on her program, Nick didn't stick around.

****

Peyton stood in the relative safety of Nick's office doorway for several seconds before he spoke. "Time to pluck that thorn from your paw, bro."

The refined sophistication of his spacious corner office belied the fact that Nick had been raised by a single father in the shadows of the Las Vegas strip, but befitted the man who was on track to become the country's most successful nightclub owner before he turned forty.

Nick and Peyton had met in college and become best friends—even though Peyton was a trust-fund legacy and Nick attended as a scholarship student. Peyton also knew Ava and had a firsthand view of how her vanishing act had knocked Nick on his ass. Two months had passed since Nick's trip to San Diego. He understood that the setup with Ava was Peyton's way of looking out for him, but he was still raw and not ready to forgive.

"Don't you mean knife from my back…bro?"

Peyton's groan was loud and dramatic. "Come on, man. You know I wasn't trying to hurt you."

Nick's gaze met Peyton's apologetic one. "What's to say you did?"

"Oh, I don't know. Maybe the fact weeks have passed and you're still grumpy and pissed?"

"That doesn't mean I'm hurt." He returned his attention to the document in front of him. "You're supposed to have my back, but you sent me in unprepared. Until I'm ready to move past that fact, you'd be wise to give me plenty of space."

"Okay, maybe I handled it wrong, but I didn't think you'd go if you knew Ava was there."

Nick's jaw tightened. "Like I said, knife…back." He glanced up. "Is that it?" The force of his displeasure vibrated through him.

Instead of retreating, Peyton squared his shoulders and stepped into the room. "I own my part, but it's not only me you're freezing out. We want to know how to fix it."

Nick frowned. "We?"

"Me." Peyton sighed and plopped down into a chair that faced Nick. "The staff—although they're clueless as to the why. They figure I know what's going on, so I drew the short straw, and…here I am."

The top floor of Nick's Las Vegas flagship, Morgan's Gold, housed the corporate office of his expanding business empire. Nick had been reclusive since his return from San Diego. He wasn't surprised his employees were concerned because most had been with him since the beginning and knew his recent behavior was uncharacteristic.

Plus, his demeanor wasn't the only thing that had changed. He'd shifted focus to Club Fête in LA, number two on their acquisitions list, and had worked like a demon to solidify the deal. Still, he wasn't about to admit it had anything to do with seeing Ava again.

"I fail to see how anyone has cause for complaint. LA was on-boarded in record time, our investors are pleased with the Seattle and Vegas sites, and bonuses have never been bigger."

"San Diego was next, not LA."

Nick's mouth twisted. "Doesn't mean LA wasn't ready."

"Anger. Denial. Sarcasm." Peyton stretched out his legs, crossed them at the ankles, and steepled his fingers on his thighs. "We both know what's going on here, Nick. The question is what are you going to do about it?"

At times Nick wished he and Peyton weren't so close. This was one. They had gone their separate ways after college—Nick in investments, Peyton in advertising. But after a couple of years, they'd both found their careers lacking and had started plans for their own business enterprise.

Since Peyton clearly wasn't in a hurry to leave, Nick put down his pen. "If you're worried about the company, don't. We will pick up San Diego."

When Peyton shook his head, Nick sighed and leaned back in his chair.

"Was it a shock seeing Ava again? Sure. But then you knew it would be, so as far as I'm concerned, the manner of your payback is the only thing that's unresolved."

"Dammit, it's Christmas, and I found Ava!" Peyton's smile was unrepentant. "The way I see it, you should be thanking me."

Doesn't mean she wants to be found.

After Nick left Club Brizo, he'd checked out of his hotel and headed home. He'd made it to Sin City in record time, and even though he was exhausted physically, he'd been too wired to sleep. Within hours, he'd completed an internet deep-dive on Ava and found that she was on track to become a tenured professor of music and volunteered as a music teacher for children living in the barrio. She was also a customer favorite at Brizo where she performed one Saturday a month.

The knowledge she was realizing her dreams

without him left Nick unsettled and vulnerable. Even if he still had feelings for her, it didn't alter reality. Ava hadn't needed him then, and she didn't need him now. His visit to Club Brizo only underscored that bitter fact.

Thanking Peyton was the last thing he wanted to do. Nick narrowed his eyes. "Ava has moved on."

"You don't know that. I didn't see a ring. Did you?"

"Dammit, Peyton, let it go."

"I can't do that, Nick." Peyton's hands sliced through the air. "We both know Ava's the reason you've spent the past few years avoiding any type of entanglement. It's not healthy."

"I date."

"Uh-huh. The occasional weekend hookup isn't my definition of a date, and it shouldn't be yours. This may be your last chance to fix things, so forget your pride and do something."

Holding on to his temper took considerable effort. "Not that my love life is your concern, but you seem to forget I'm not the one who wouldn't commit."

Peyton shook his head. "I haven't forgotten. In fact, I remember that I warned you when you bought the ring Ava wasn't ready. Face it, Nick. You tried to steamroll her, and she bolted."

He bristled, and his hands fisted. "Go to hell, Peyton."

"No thanks, brother." Peyton shot to his feet and stalked to the door. "One of us is already there…but he's too big of an ass to see it."

After Peyton left, the remainder of the afternoon passed in a blur, and Nick accomplished little. Disgusted with his lack of focus, he jammed a stack of files into his briefcase and left his office. He stopped at his assistant's desk, told Christine to handle his calls, and headed to his car. When the drive home failed to soothe his fragmented emotions, he fixed himself a generous drink, lit a fire—more for effect than heat—and spent the next hours staring into the flames. Eventually, his anger with Peyton began to cool, but the memories kept coming.

Once Ava responded to the messages he left with Fusion's bartender, they had agreed to meet for coffee at a trendy downtown café. When he attended her performance, her songs had soothed his soul and tugged at his heart. What her presence did to his body when she sat down across from him wasn't as noble.

She wore street clothes with as much panache as she had her club attire. Her ebony hair flowed midway down the back of her strappy, peach-colored sundress, white sandals exposed pretty toenail polish that matched her fingernails, and the light scent of musk hovered in the air whenever she moved. They made small talk until their coffee was delivered, and once she took her first sip, he made his pitch.

"You're a tremendous talent, Ava. I'm sure you've been told—with your looks and voice—you could go far. But my sources tell me you don't have representation. May I ask why?"

"I don't need it."

He thought her words a negotiating gambit and played along. "I think you do, and I'd love to sign you on. I'm opening my own club soon, so I haven't taken on a new client in months, but you're special." He recognized the look she shot him, and shook his head. "Sounds cliché, I know. But headlining at Fusion and an impressive following on social media is just a start."

She set her cup down and smiled. "I'm sure you're

good at what you do, Nick, but I'm not interested in a career in show business. My music is very personal to me. Just now it pays the bills, but that's as public as I care to go."

When it sank in that she was serious, he was stunned. Instead of dimming his interest, however, his personal attraction grew. He took her hand in his, absorbed the jolt that shot through him, and pivoted.

"People with half your God-given abilities would sell a kidney for bright lights and fame. I realize you don't owe me a damn thing, but I'd love to know how you envision your future."

She looked down at their joined hands, tipped up her chin, and met the directness of his gaze with her own. "I'm going to continue my volunteer work with inner-city children, work at Fusion to pay my bills, and finish my dissertation. After that, I'll find a music program that suits me and become a music professor."

Her expression read only openness and resolve.

"No shit?"

She nodded. "No shit."

"Then why agree to meet with me?"

She shrugged and smiled. "You made quite an impression on our bartender, and you're very persistent. My curiosity got the better of me."

Her smile, flirty, full of humor, and an underlying wholesomeness took his breath away. "To be honest, I'm glad that it did. Even though it stings on one level, I can live with the dent to my professional pride."

"Oh?" Her head tilted to the side. "I'm disappointed. I thought you'd put up more of a fight."

"Normally I would, but…" He leaned forward, stroked a finger across the delicate bones of her wrist, and held her tawny gaze. "I have a strict policy…I don't date the talent."

Her eyes widened just before she laughed, a low husky sound that rippled down his spine to pool in his gut. Just like that, he was a goner. By the end of their third date, Nick's dream of building a world-class entertainment empire had expanded to include Ava at his side.

For months their relationship deepened on an emotional and physical connection that was as binding as it was intense. By the following spring, he'd enticed her away from Fusion to feature at the newly opened Morgan's Gold. Ava completed, defended, and published her dissertation and started applying to music programs for teaching opportunities.

Unwilling to wait any longer to make their relationship permanent, Nick had proposed on Christmas morning. She had accepted but wanted to wait until her career was on track before they planned a wedding. With no clear idea how long that would be, Nick had exploded.

He cringed at the memory of the epic fight that had followed, but he'd been too angry at what he perceived as rejection. The battle had ended when he issued an ultimatum and stormed out.

By the time he'd cooled off, she was gone.

He set his empty glass down, crossed to the hidden safe behind the bar, and took out the box that held Ava's ring. He'd thought about getting rid of the ring numerous times, but each time something held him back. It was time he figured out what that something was.

****

Ava shut off the lights of the empty auditorium, the silence heavy after the colorful Tuesday evening holiday pageant that ended an hour ago. It was the first time her students had participated in the annual event, and she couldn't be prouder of their eagerness and talent.

She'd moved to San Diego to realize her dreams on her own terms, even though her determination resulted in heartache that still resonated, especially at Christmas. Born in Carson City, she didn't remember the drug-addict parents who'd abandoned her to the Nevada foster care system when she was four. She was nine when her mother died from a heroin overdose and her father disappeared. Months later, she was cleared for legal adoption, but adoption at the ripe age of ten was rare.

She was no exception.

A year after she became a permanent ward of the state, she was relocated from the group foster home in Carson City to a state-sponsored residence hall in Las Vegas. There she met Juanita Canaday, a retired music teacher who volunteered at the facility. Mrs. Canaday brought sound and color to Ava's world and nurtured an untapped passion for music Ava hadn't known existed.

Ava proved to be as gifted as she was enthusiastic. Not only did Mrs. Canaday become her mentor, but she was the closest Ava had come to having a mother. For once, Ava's life was full of support and possibilities. At fifteen, she blossomed into the role of lead soloist in her high school's choral ensemble and eventually earned full tuition to the Nevada Institute of Music. She was a fellowship scholar working on her doctorate when she met and fell in love with Nick Morgan.

Their relationship had been intense, but short-lived. Since their breakup, Ava had shied away from intimate entanglements. Devoting her time and energies to the many facets of her craft proved enough, except during the holiday season when her university and community center classes were on hiatus. Then a bittersweet loneliness would dog her steps, and she would count off the days until the new year arrived and her world was back to normal.

If her life choices left her occasionally melancholy, she pushed through. So she fought the impulse to feel sorry for herself and took a deep breath. Christmas was four days away, and even if she was alone, she had much to celebrate. Not only was there Christmas morning—when she and center staff would hand out presents to the neighborhood children—she was headlining Club Brizo's New Year's Eve party.

Ava turned onto her street, marveled at the jolly decorations on display, and smiled. She was an independent, successful woman who had beat the odds to create the warm and cozy home that awaited her. All that was missing were her own festive trimmings. Resolve to remedy that circumstance lightened her steps as she headed inside. Tomorrow she'd get a tree, dust off her ornaments, and bake her favorite Christmas cookies—something she hadn't done since she'd left Vegas.

Wednesday morning dawned with the promise of sunshine and temperatures in the mid-sixties. After spending an hour at a nearby tree lot, Ava arranged for her purchases to be delivered and stopped at her local market on her way home. Soon after her groceries were put away and her purchases unpacked, the tree arrived and was set up in the living room.

She tuned in to an all-holiday satellite music station, poured a generous glass of wine, unfurled and positioned her new tree lights, and plugged them in. Pleased with her efforts, she grabbed the wine and headed to her kitchen. The rest of the tree decorations would wait until her signature candy cane sandwich cookies were baking in the oven and the minty-chocolate scent of the cookie shells mingled with the tree's unique fragrance.

Sixty-four minutes later, her kitchen was the site of controlled chaos. Ava had discovered the pleasures of cooking when she moved into her first apartment. She was an exuberant, messy cook whose counters were now covered with the fallout. Content and singing along to a popular carol, she took the cookie shells out of the refrigerator where she'd placed them to chill, set the trays in the oven, and activated the timer.

After she taste tested the peppermint-buttercream filling—twice—she turned her attention to the cleanup. She nailed a high note, executed an enthusiastic twirl, and knocked over the half-full tin of flour.

Undeterred by the cloud of white dust that billowed out, she swiveled toward the miniscule utility room and her handy broom. When her right foot skidded on the coated tile, she grabbed at the counter to balance herself—only to have her left foot shoot out from under her and pitch her forward. Sharp pain arced through her head, bright light exploded before her eyes, and everything went dark.

Ava rebelled against the shrill, insistent sound that grated on the periphery of her consciousness. The strident noise twisted and merged with the incessant pounding in her head, even as an acrid smell assailed her. She opened her eyes and blinked her surroundings into focus, but several seconds more passed before she registered her sprawled position on the cold, gritty tile of her kitchen floor.

As reality returned, she tried to sit up. The room pitched, her head hurt, and her stomach roiled. She groaned, clutched her abdomen with one hand, and touched the robin's-egg-sized lump on her temple with the other. Once the room settled, she got to her feet, chucked the charred remains of her chocolate cookie shells into the trash, and turned off the timer.

But the racket resumed.

It took a few moments more before she realized that the cacophony was coming from the doorbell. "Ugh!" She dusted herself off as best she could, used her fingers to arrange her hair across her battered forehead, and headed to her front door.

"Com—ouch!" When the pain increased with the sound of her own voice, she shut her mouth and moved as quickly as she could to get to her visitor before the summons blasted out again.

****

Nick dropped his hand to his side as the door opened. The internal battle that waged since his visit to Club Brizo had continued while he called in several markers, packed, and got into his car. So, when Ava appeared in the doorway—with white dust splattered over her hair, skin, and clothes—he braced himself. All manner of scenarios had played out on the long drive to San Diego, but not one imagined the sparkle in her amber eyes or the wide grin that suddenly dimpled her cheeks.

"You're here!"

His hands clamped around her forearms when she launched herself at him, but the instinct to tread carefully didn't fully take hold. In the space of a single, slow-motion heartbeat, the emptiness of the last two years disintegrated, and he pulled her in. When her lips fastened onto his, he wrapped his arms securely around her and accepted what was offered.

As desire swiftly roared through him, he backed her across the threshold, kicked the door closed, and immersed himself in the familiar mating of their tongues and the feel of her body moving intimately against his. Eager to reclaim every inch of her, he relinquished her mouth to forge a heated trail of rediscovery across the line of her jaw and the rapid beat of her pulse.

The deep well of need threatened his control. "God, I missed you."

"Me, too." Her words were low and muffled as her lips explored the taut column of his neck. "You've been gone a couple weeks, but it feels like forever."

"I'm here now—*wait*—weeks?" He took a step back but didn't release her. "What are—?" His words died when his gaze settled on the red, puffy skin perilously close to one eye. "Ava, did you hit your head?"

"I must have." She grimaced. "I'm hoping it looks better than it feels."

"You…?" Foreboding hit him like a blow to the gut. "You don't remember?"

"Not exactly." She shrugged. "I woke up on the floor to the smell of burning Christmas cookies, so the children will have to wait until next year to try them."

He stiffened, released his hold, and took a quick scan of the room. "Children?"

"Did you forget we're distributing gifts and goodies at the center on Christmas morning?" She glanced down at his hands. "And why didn't you bring in your luggage?"

"My luggage?" His mind reeled as he tried to keep up.

She slanted him a look. "We agreed we'd spend the holiday at my place."

His thoughts cleared as understanding dawned. That had been their plan—two years ago. "Yes, we did." His hand gently swept back her hair, and she flinched. "But first, we're getting this checked out."

"Don't be silly."

When she tried to pull away, he gripped her hand and tugged her back. "I'm serious, Ava. Is everything turned off in the kitchen?"

"Yes, but—"

"No buts. Head injuries are nothing to play with. Where's your purse?"

"Nick." She plucked at his hold, irritation edging her words. "I don't have time for this."

"We'll make time." His tone softened at her rebellious glare. "I want nothing more than to be here with you, but I'm worried, babe. Do it for me?"

"Oh…fine!" She grabbed her handbag and snatched up her keys from the small table by the front door. "But if we end up spending your first night back waiting to be told you're overreacting, it's on you."

Her snit lasted as long as it took for them to get settled in his car. He was about to push the start button when her slender hand reached for his.

"I'm sorry."

He took her hand, turned her palm up, and raised it to his lips. "No need to apologize. Just remember I want what's best for you. Okay?"

She squeezed his hand. "Okay."

He released his hold, pulled out his cell phone, and programmed the route to the nearest hospital. Once they registered at the ER desk, he performed a cursory check of her under the guise of removing most of what turned out to be flour from her hair and skin. No further signs of injury were evident, even though he didn't need a medical degree to figure out the blow to her head had messed with her memory.

Once Ava signed permission to allow him to accompany her, they were summoned to the back. Nick sat in a chair in the corner of the room while Ava was examined. Her responses to the doctor's questions were succinct, but not all of her answers were current. Concern tightened his chest and ran a loop of dire outcomes through his mind. Nick snapped back to the present with the doctor's concluding words.

"From what you've said, you were out for more than five minutes, Ava," Dr. Ritzie observed. "I believe you may have a Grade III concussion, but I'll confirm my diagnosis once I've ordered a few tests."

Ava's shoulders slumped. "Then I can go home, right?"

"I'll know more when I get the results, but standard protocol is an overnight stay for observation."

"But it's the holidays, and Nick just got back!"

"Let's not get excited yet." Dr. Ritzie patted Ava's knee. "Nothing's final until I review your labs."

"If my tests are normal and I promise to follow your instructions, you'll let me leave?"

Dr. Ritzie shook her head. "We'll see. Best case I can release you, but only if someone keeps an eye on you for the next few days."

Ava perked up. "Then it's lucky Nick returned when he did. He loves to boss me around."

Ouch. He returned Ava's smile, but her words stung. Maybe Peyton was right, and he had pushed her too hard.

He dug deep to keep his tone light. "When you face-plant trying to bake cookies, you get what you get."

Dr. Ritzie chuckled. "I'll order those tests. In the meantime, I need you to relax…but no napping until we know more."

Nick waited until the physician took two pillows from a metal cabinet and propped them behind Ava before he stood up.

"Behave while I have a word with the good doctor," he told Ava. He followed Dr. Ritzie out, closed the curtain behind them, and motioned for her to put some distance between them and Ava's cubicle.

Once they were several feet away, she faced him. "There isn't more I can tell you until after the test results, Nick."

"And I appreciate that, Doctor, but there's something you should know. I listened to Ava's responses. Although she's been lucid since I came on the scene, some of the details of this Christmas appear to be mixed up with previous ones."

"Can you elaborate?"

He nodded. "I just came in from Las Vegas. Ava thinks it was Chicago. That and a couple other things she's said makes me believe she's blending our Christmas two years ago with this year."

"Well, that does complicate matters." Her expression wasn't encouraging as she made notations on Ava's paperwork. "With a minor concussion, concerning issues usually show up within twenty-four hours. Selective amnesia isn't typical, though, so it extends how long we need to be on guard. I'll arrange for a room."

His heart sank. "Is that our only option here, Dr. Ritzie?"

Her expression sharpened. "Are you asking if you can still take her home?"

"Yes, ma'am. Ava was in foster care growing up and didn't get much chance to celebrate. She loves everything about Christmas, and having to spend it confined in a hospital would upset her more than most. I believe I can take care of her needs myself, but I'll arrange for a private-care nurse if that's what it takes to get her discharged."

The doctor's gaze on his was steady. "What's usually best in these situations is for the patient to avoid stressors and get plenty of rest and TLC. To recuperate in a familiar, comfortable environment is the ideal. In Ava's case, it's imperative she stay calm, get plenty of rest, and not be left alone for at least forty-eight hours. She will also need follow-up care. With the holidays it's unlikely she'll get an appointment before Monday, which is the reason I'm even considering your offer. Are you sure you want to take this on?"

He didn't hesitate. "Yes, ma'am, I am."

"Well, then." The doctor paused and pursed her lips. "If her tests come back clean and she agrees, I'll release her into your care. If her memory hasn't returned by the time she sees her regular physician, more tests will be ordered. But if she experiences any interim pain or distress, you must immediately bring her back here."

He nodded. "You have my word we'll follow your directions to the letter."

The doctor's penetrating gaze held his. "You care for her a great deal."

Something inside of him shifted, and the truth of her words settled over him like a warm, familiar blanket. He nodded. "I have the ring to prove it."

"Good man." Dr. Ritzie smiled, tucked her pen in her pocket, and patted his arm. "Then let's order those tests and hope for the best."

Night had fallen when Ava and Nick left the hospital. Ava had been poked, prodded, X-rayed, and prodded some more, but she'd handled it without complaint. On the way to her house, Nick stopped at a nearby drive-through while she rested her head back against her seat and closed her eyes. He used the respite to navigate the unfamiliar city and process the monumental events of the day.

He'd been unable to settle after his confrontation with Peyton and, after a restless night, had left for San Diego at dawn. Thoughts of Ava alone and injured tightened his chest, clenched his gut, and left him grateful to whatever whims of fate had brought him to her doorstep that afternoon.

He parked behind Ava's car, turned off the ignition, and softly touched her face. "How are you holding up?"

"Fine." She wrinkled her nose and opened her eyes. "Although this isn't how I wanted to spend our Christmas." Her gaze skittered off his as she turned to look out her window at the inflated elves in her neighbor's yard. One shoulder lifted. "Now everything is ruined."

"Don't think like that." He kept his voice level. "You've had a rough time, but we have three days to get you back in the holiday spirit. Dr. Ritzie said you could even see your students Christmas morning…as long as you take it easy until then."

"I know." She looked down at her hands. "I guess I'm just feeling…off."

He covered her hands with his. "Even with that

goose egg on your head and your plans curtailed, I promise you everything will turn out fine. Now let's get you inside. We don't want our dinner to get cold."

Nick had hoped she'd perk up once she'd eaten. Instead she looked lost, vulnerable, and ready to shatter into pieces. As soon as they'd finished their meal, he lifted her into his arms to carry her upstairs. He waited outside her bathroom while she washed up and stayed close until she climbed into bed.

When he bent over and tucked her in, she sighed and reached up to stroke his cheek. "You cut short your business trip only to spend hours in a hospital emergency room and eat lukewarm takeout. This isn't how I envisioned your homecoming."

He twisted his head and kissed her palm. "I'm here, and you're going to recover. That's all that matters."

"I know, I know." She gingerly shook her head. "I've never seen this side of you."

He frowned. Dr. Ritzie had repeated the importance of following her instructions numerous times. He was to wake her every three hours, ask her a list of questions, and ensure that she was coherent before he let her go back to sleep.

"Are you worried I can't take care of you?"

Ava was shaking her head before he finished speaking. "Not at all. I'm pissy because I hurt, I can't take a decent bath for forty-eight hours, and I feel like a stranger in my own skin."

He straightened and shoved his hands into his pockets. "I'm sure what you're feeling is as normal as it is…temporary."

"I suppose." She met his gaze. "You've been wonderful, Nick. Don't give up on me."

He held the connection for several moments before he spoke. "Never."

His words hung in the air for several moments before she smiled and relaxed against the pillows.

"Good to know. It's your turn to get settled. I don't know about you, but I'm ready to put this day behind us."

Even though his body ached with the need that flooded him, Nick skimmed a chaste kiss across Ava's warm lips and grabbed his overnight kit. Doubt crowded in the moment the bathroom door shut behind him.

What had started out as a quest for answers had spun into an ever-growing web of half-truths. That, and the fact her memory could return at any time, made it foolish to pretend his subterfuge wasn't going to blow up in his face. But he couldn't regret his duplicity. For precious moments he'd held her in his arms, once again felt her love and desire, and finally acknowledged how much his stubborn pride had cost him.

Two years ago she'd accused him of thinking only of himself.

She'd been right.

Still, wallowing and self-flagellation wasn't his scene, so his reckoning would have to wait. As he saw it, he had two options. He could hire a private duty nurse, come clean, and beg for forgiveness, or he could keep his mouth shut and take care of her himself.

He didn't ponder his choices for long, because the thought of leaving Ava in another's care was unacceptable. He would stay the course and lavish her with the support and attention she deserved for as long as he could. He only hoped she remembered his efforts when her memory returned.

The decision made, he finished his nighttime routine

and walked into her bedroom. Two things registered simultaneously and made him smile. She was sound asleep…and she still took up most of the bed.

He set his watch alarm for two hours, pulled back the cover, and slid in. Carefully, he nudged her over until he was in, turned off the bedside lamp, and closed his eyes.

****

The rise and fall of soothing waves rocked her, a steady, distant drumbeat pulsed in her ear, and a pleasant breeze soothed the skin of her face. Ava opened her eyes to the subtle movement of Nick's chest, the warm flow of his exhalations, and the steady rhythm of his heart. She smiled, lifted her hand toward the taut skin of his abdomen…and froze mid-motion.

The room tilted as panic and confusion swamped her senses. A quick jab of pain redirected her hand to the tenderness beside her left eye even as lightning-fast memories tumbled through her mind on a wave of nausea. She took in slow, deep breaths until the discomfort subsided…and remembered everything.

She'd slipped and hit her head…and Nick had appeared and taken her to the hospital. The return of her memory didn't answer why he'd been at her door in the first place, but he'd pretended he was still her boyfriend and gotten her released from the hospital. He'd even complied with her doctor's directives and awakened her like clockwork during the night.

Why?

Careful not to wake him, she edged her head off his shoulder onto her own pillow and examined the face of the only man she had ever loved. He seemed thinner, the angles of his face were sharper, and…were those strands of silver nestled in the lush thickness of his hair?

Rapid-fire emotions detonated inside her—anger, hurt, and a grief so profound she trembled. The arm that anchored her to Nick's side tightened, and he mumbled something unintelligible. She lay motionless until his breathing evened out again, replayed the last twenty-four hours, and cringed with embarrassment.

He must have thought she'd lost her mind when she first opened the door. Not only had she been thrilled to see him, but she'd kissed him! And he'd kissed her back…just before he insisted they go to the hospital.

Why would he do any of that?

Her gaze travelled over the expanse of bare skin— skin that stopped at the low waistband of his pajama bottoms—and marveled at this unfamiliar side of Nick. She was no closer to deciphering what it all meant when the alarm signaled.

His eyes opened, his gaze softened when it met hers, and he smiled. "How do you feel?"

With the blinders lifted, she drank in the sight of his familiar features and wondered how best to tell him her memory had returned. Her pulse quickened. "Better."

"And your head?" he asked as he propped himself up, gingerly brushed her hair back, and examined the bruised skin.

At his touch, heat pooled in her belly. "Umm." She cleared her throat and concentrated on his question. "A bit tender, but the pain is almost gone."

His gaze held hers. "Any nausea?"

She prevaricated. "Not anymore."

"The good doctor would be pleased." He leaned down and kissed her nose. "You didn't eat much last night. Think you can manage breakfast?"

"Umm, yeah. I think so."

He was silent for several moments as his gaze searched hers. "You sure everything's okay?"

She felt like a deer must when caught in bright headlights. In the silence that followed, the loneliness and loss of the past months crowded into her mind and made her decision. Right or wrong, she wanted this reprieve for as long as possible.

She nodded. "Just a little tired."

"Well, you'll have the day in bed to get your energy back."

Guilt lifted its guileful head. "I can come downstairs."

"Not a chance, champ." He pressed a quick kiss to her lips and rolled out of bed. "How does tea, toast, and a couple of scrambled eggs sound?" He stood up and grabbed an undershirt from an open bag on the chair.

The sight of his near-naked body added to the havoc. She wasn't sure she could keep anything down, and it wasn't all due to her injury. "Maybe just coffee."

He shook his head and turned back toward the bed, his muscles flexing as he slipped the cotton over his head. "Try again."

Her breath stuttered in her throat. "Umm, tea and toast?"

He crossed back to the bed, leaned down, and tipped her chin up. "You need sustenance to heal. Tea, toast, and one egg."

Her pout was automatic. "Fine."

He flashed her a cocky grin and walked out the door. True to his word, she did little all day but eat, watch television, doze, and battle her conscience. Even so, exhaustion overtook her halfway through dinner. She was asleep by the time Nick returned from cleaning up the kitchen.

She woke Christmas Eve morning riddled with self-reproach and Nick nowhere to be seen. She had no idea when he had come to bed, but at least his forty-eight-hour watch was almost over. Restricted to one more basin bath, she finished her ablutions, donned capri leggings and a sporty top, and left her bedroom. When she reached the stairs, Nick was coming up.

He shook his head and scooped her up to carry her down the steps. She saw the boxes of decorations stacked around the almost-bare tree the instant they entered the living room. Overjoyed, she squeezed his neck and planted a noisy kiss on his cheek.

"What was that?"

"A thank you." She paused and chose her next words cautiously. "You've gone out of your way to take care of me, even though I'm pretty sure this isn't how you wanted to spend your holiday break."

"Hmm." He removed the arm beneath her legs but kept his arm around her shoulders. The result was her slow slide down the length of his hard body. Once her feet touched the floor and she was on firm footing, his hands migrated to her waist. "You know how the unexpected can scare the hell out of you and show you what's really important?"

Her response was barely more than a whisper. "Yes."

"That's what these last two days have been for me. I'm glad you're in my life, even though I'm damn sure I've done a poor job demonstrating it."

His gaze pinned hers as he lowered his head. She stretched onto her toes and met him halfway. Where before his kisses were almost platonic, this one simmered with heat. Long-denied need burst through, and the years between them melted away. She struggled to calm her labored breathing when the kiss ended, certain that his stunned expression was a reflection of her own.

When he feathered a gentle salute across the skin of her forehead, she dared to hope. If ever there was a time to confess, it was now.

"Nick, I need to—"

He pressed a finger against her parted lips and shook his head. "Get some food in your belly?"

"No…I mean, yes…but—"

"No buts." He ushered her to a high stool at one end of the breakfast bar. "It's Christmas Eve and time we got down to business."

The urge to come clean subsided as she watched him move with ease around her small kitchen. "What do you mean?"

He grinned and walked to the refrigerator. "You're going to need an abundance of both energy and patience because I'm going to decorate our tree. With your help, of course."

Our tree. The Nick she remembered was alpha male and had given her no reason to believe he had a single sentimental or domestic cell in his body. In fact, he hadn't bothered with a tree of his own and had dismissed her holiday preparations as excessive. No way was she going to ruin the moment.

Once they'd eaten breakfast, he helped her settle on the sofa and plugged in the tree. Her awe at this accommodating side of him was short-lived when he popped the lid off a box, selected an ornate ribbon, and turned to drape it on the tree.

Horrified, she quashed what remained of her conscience and committed fully to a Christmas cover-up. "Nick! Everyone knows the ornaments go on next."

****

Nick wiggled his eyebrows. "Apparently not."

Ava giggled, and the tension he'd been carrying since he woke up to the intimate press of her body against his began to level. The skin on her head, though colorful, was almost smooth, and he'd noted no further indications of pain. He was determined to make her recovery as quick and easy as possible, even if that meant it also shortened the time left with her.

"Don't tell me you never decorated a Christmas tree before."

He shrugged, set the ribbon aside, and grabbed a box of fancy bulbs. "Never had to…that was Dad's thing." He rocked back onto his heels. He rarely spoke of his parents, but his mother had died of breast cancer when he was seven, and his father had died of a heart attack while Nick was working his way through college. "After Mom passed, Dad made sure we had a tree and, even though we didn't have much money, at least a pair of socks and a toy for me under it on Christmas morning."

"I'm sorry I didn't have a chance to know them."

"Me, too. I guess that leaves you to teach me the fine art of tree trimming."

What followed was over an hour of Ava's heavy-handed directing, plenty of eye-rolling on his part, and lots of laughter. Once the tree met her exacting standards, he heated up the remains of a chicken casserole he found in the fridge and arranged their meal on the coffee table. When her eyes began to droop, he coaxed her into taking a nap while he fired up his laptop and checked in on the office.

He returned emails and rescheduled next week's appointments but found it hard to concentrate with her so near. Peyton was right. He had taken Ava for granted long before she turned down his proposal. Once she did, arrogance and pride had taken over.

After her nap, she wheedled and cajoled until he agreed to try his hand at baking. From her perch on a kitchen stool, she orchestrated his every move until a dozen candy cane sandwich cookies cooled on the counters. And with each smile, the warmth inside him grew. By the time she took her first excited bite, he knew he would never willingly live without her again.

They ordered pizza from Ava's favorite Italian restaurant for dinner. When she leaned across the table to wipe a spatter of sauce from his chin—and steal a plump mushroom off his plate—memories of similar antics returned full force. Now, as he waited for her to finish her first shower in days, recollections of her wet and willing crowded in as well.

For the hundredth time, he reminded himself she was still recuperating. As much as he ached to finish what their earlier kiss promised, he couldn't allow his needs to endanger her recovery. The sight of her wrapped only in matching towels over her hair and torso tested that resolve. He consigned to memory her inviting smile and provocative image and got to his feet.

Her gaze tracked to the overnight bag in his hand, and her smile wobbled. "What's going on?"

"Now that the forty-eight hours are over, I figured you'd rest better if I sleep in the spare bedroom."

She frowned. "I've slept fine with you here."

"Yes, well." He cleared his throat and opted for honesty. "The truth is I'll rest better if I sleep in the spare room."

Red stained her cheeks. "I didn't realize you were uncomfortable."

Comprehension dawned. "You misunderstand. It's not the sleeping part that's…hard." The shift in her expression was almost comical. "I'm no saint, Ava. I'm glad you've gotten the respite you need, but with each second that passes, it becomes more challenging not to peel off your clothes and sink inside you."

He was halfway to the door when she touched the center of his back.

"Nick."

"I'll be fine. There are things we need to discuss, but not ton—"

His words sputtered to a stop when a pair of delicate hands reached around his shoulders and dropped damp towels on the floor at his feet.

He groaned. "The doctor said—"

"—to take it easy and relax. We've followed those orders for two days, and I feel fine. Besides, I hear making love can be very relaxing. Rejuvenating even."

He groaned again, twisted to haul her damp body against his, and buried his face in the fragrant waves of hair. "Honey, I know you think—"

She stopped his words with a kiss so full of passion and need a shudder ripped through him. When she rocked back on her heels, took hold of his hand, and pivoted, he drank in the naked femininity of her beauty like a man dying of thirst.

Her curves were rounder and her hair considerably longer, but not much else had changed—including his body's intense reaction to her. He followed the smooth expanse of her swaying backside as the last sliver of restraint snapped.

"You fight dirty."

"No, Nick." Her chuckle was low and seductive. "I fight to win."

****

The heady power of being in charge lasted until Ava reached the bed. The next instant, she was flat on her back on top of the duvet. She opened her mouth to protest, only to shut it again when Nick tugged his shirt over his head, tossed it over his shoulder, and reached for the snap on his jeans.

Heat parched her throat and weakened her knees when his familiar weight covered her seconds later. His tender lips and hands forged trails of arousal so reckless with hunger shockwaves of desire racked her writhing body.

Just when she thought she would burst with pleasure, he rolled away.

"Protection," he rasped, as he gulped in air.

"What?"

"My bag. There's protection in the overnight box in the front pocket, but I'm going to need a minute."

"You've got fifteen, maybe twenty seconds."

Without an ounce of self-consciousness, she scrambled off the bed, picked up the bag by the door, and upended the contents on the carpet. Only when the pure maleness of his laughter reached her did embarrassment loom. Moments later she straightened to her full, nude glory—a small carton in hand—paced to the foot of the bed, and stopped.

"What the hell is so funny, Nick Morgan?"

"Never you, honey."

"Then explain yourself, or this"—she held up the black and gold-embossed package—"is going back where it came from. Unopened."

"But my twenty seconds are up."

When he caught up to her, her snit had taken her halfway across the room.

"Okay, okay! I wasn't laughing at you. Come back to bed."

She didn't resist when he turned her around. "Not until you tell me what was so humorous."

"Not humor…relief. I'm so aroused by you I was afraid I would hurt you. So I hit slow in a bid for control, and you"—he ran his hands down her sides and cupped her derriere—"spring into action like a warrior goddess who wants no quarter."

"Hmmm." She tipped her chin and sniffed. "Well, maybe you ruined the moment and now I've changed my mind."

He laughed, lifted her high, and clamped his arms around her hips. "Allow me to change it back." With unerring aim, he pulled a nipple into his mouth and suckled. When his skilled lips eventually released its mate, tiny whimpers escaped her throat.

"Ready to come back to bed now?"

The sun was up when a sated and content Ava stretched, turned over, and connected with Nick's heavy-lidded gaze. Fragments of a night full of love and laughter flooded her mind, and suddenly, the enormity of the deceit between them was more than she could bear.

His hand was an inch from her breast when she stiffened.

He froze. "Did I hurt you? Are you in pain?"

"No! No." She shook her head, refusing to be distracted by the expanse of skin and sinew. "Nothing like that."

"Then what's going on?"

"I have to tell you something."

"All right." He sat up. "I'm listening."

"Nick, my memory returned…the morning after my accident."

She watched the play of emotions—was that fear?—and something undecipherable chase across his handsome features and prayed she could weather the storm that was sure to come. But nothing could have prepared her for the words that barely parted his lips.

"I know."

****

Siren sat at the piano in Club Brizo on New Year's Eve and played her final song of the night. Dressed in a gold lamé mini dress and her signature black stilettos, she lifted her right hand and signaled to the audience. As the bridge of "Auld Lang Syne" rang out, the spotlight expanded to cover the entire stage.

Gene, the club manager, stepped up to the standing mic and made a show of checking his watch before he spoke. "Well, folks, it's getting to be that time. Does everyone have their drink in hand?"

A crystal flute of champagne appeared over her left shoulder as cheers reverberated around the packed room and strobe lights began to flash. As she reached for the glass, light danced off the sparkle on her finger just as a familiar form slid onto the bench beside her.

She thought back to Christmas morning as she awaited Nick's reaction to her confession. Instead of anger and rejection, he'd assuaged her guilt with love and grace.

"I already figured that out," he'd said calmly. "You're not a good liar, honey…your expression tells on you every time. It's why I warn you never to play poker. I knew when I woke up Thursday morning and caught you staring at me."

She was stunned. "Why didn't you say anything?"

"I needed more time with you." He shrugged. "And I convinced myself the only reason you pretended was because you still love me."

She punched his shoulder. "You think you're so smart."

He shook his head. "Not smart enough to understand how you felt two years ago. But I promise I've learned my lesson."

Later, they dressed and drove to the center. Nick volunteered on the refreshment serving line while Ava assisted Santa with the gaily wrapped packages and the legion of children that swarmed the auditorium. When they returned home, he settled her on the sofa, dropped to one knee, pulled out her original ring box, and proposed.

This time when she said yes, she had no reservations or doubts. From that moment, her life had been filled with love and laughter, heart-to-heart conversations, and mind-bending sex.

As for their future, Nick had decided he would split his time between Vegas and San Diego while he groomed a manager for Morgan's Gold. Peyton would manage Seattle and LA, and any further expansion had been tabled for at least a year.

Nick nuzzled the exposed line of her neck and pulled her back to the present. "Where did you go?"

"Christmas morning and everything that's happened since. Are you sure you're not going to regret moving to San Diego?"

"I am sure. Besides, Peyton has been whining about more responsibility for months, and it's about time he earned his big paycheck." The countdown began, and Nick raised her left hand to his lips. "Your turn. Any regrets?"

Ava smiled, leaned into his solid warmth, and kissed him. As the new year rang in, she raised her glass to meet his. "Not a one."

Gingerbread Men and Toad's Wart

by

Daniel Kamin

Christmas Cookies

Dedication

To my family—
To my wife, Hishge, who's always there to support me in any way possible and is cheering me on.
To my son, John, and daughter, Victoria, who do their very best to give me time to write.
And to my mother, who actually does give me time to work by helping watch the kids.
Thanks for all you do.

Standing a grand total of a finger-length tall, the gingerbread man seemed confused.

Cresella brushed a strand of dark hair under her pointed hat and sucked in a long—a very, very long—breath. "Now, I'm going to count to three…again. And by the time I reach three, you'd better be in that basket." She pointed to the picnic basket emblazoned with *Cresella's Cookies and Fineries* in silver lettering on the side.

Cookies were not known for their arithmetic skills. Chemistry, yes, which should've meant some innate ability to do simple math, but of all the cookies Cresella had baked over the years, she'd yet to find one that could add two and two, let alone count.

The little voice squeaked, "You can't catch me! I'm a gingerbread man!"

From on top of her wood-burning stove—the oven door open and the embers still hot—the gingerbread man looked out over the tree hollow she lived in and grinned.

And then it was *off*.

Down and past the kitchen, jumping around the small key stand near the door where her smartphone flashed with a message and heading to the other side of the room where her bed and cauldron lay. Right to where she had left a crack of a window open, the cold December air slithering in with bits of snow.

"Not *another* escapee," she groaned, dodging the ingredients that hung from the ceiling like bats. A bag of toad's wart smacked her in the face, and she yelped and moved around it. *Just* about going to reach the little thing, and—

A scaled jaw launched out from under the bed, and though the gingerbread man was fast, it wasn't as fast as a basilisk. A few chews. The glimmer of yellow, oh-so-happy eyes.

"Bruno!" She placed her hands on her hips. "*What* have I told you about eating our business to the ground? I can barely break even these days!" She sighed. "And with you, we'll be done for in a month's time." She leaned forward, trying to get a look under her bed. "Get out. I'm waiting."

Her familiar crawled out, slow enough he could've been an injured snake, and turned his eyes to the ground.

"Look at me."

His gaze met hers.

"The gingerbread man was going to get away, is that right, huh? So that gives you permission to eat it?"

He lifted a paw of razor-sharp claws.

"You were doing me a favor? Really, Bruno? Really? Now I'm going to have to bake another batch—and we don't have the time or money for that."

Bruno waddled off to the foot of the bed and curled up on his folded quilt.

She spun around. "I heard that, by the way. Those cookies can't figure out math, and you can't remember I can hear every word you think." She shook her head. "I swear you'd be more useful as ingredients."

With another sigh—a long, long one—she went back to work. Flour and sugar, a bit of orange toadstool, baking soda and ginger, brown sugar, molasses, some cinnamon, great spider hair, and a tad, just the smallest tad, of unicorn horn. She rolled the dough and stared out through the kitchen window, the snowflakes almost like props, not wanting to fall, just hanging in the air.

When the first snows began, her business swung into full force. That always surprised her to no end. Though maybe it shouldn't have.

While the witches in the Hollows were busy during the usual time of year—Halloween—scaring humans who crossed into the Thicket Beyond, stirring up potions that bubbled and letting out cackling laughs—all for a substantial fee, of course—Cresella could never get a business going that time of year. Humans seemed to be drawn to her for more…humanish things. Like making cute cookies that could move.

For a while, she'd run a decent business. Not as good as the scary, witchy things like flying brooms and bubbling potions, but it'd mostly paid the bills and kept her happy. Recently, though, sales just weren't what they used to be, even during her supposed boom times. A few more months of this, and she wasn't sure what she'd do.

Washing her hands off, she glanced down at her pale, whitish skin. If her cookie business did fail, how would she ever be able to do a more "witch-like" thing?

Where the other witches had skin as green as an orc's, she was pale and creamy, and while most witches, even if young, looked to be a hundred, she was both young and *looked* it. The horror of it. And the other witches in the Hollows, well, they didn't miss a chance to make sure she knew about it.

Only one witch had never paid heed to Cresella's creamy, pale skin, to her young features and lack of a hooked, mole-pocked nose. When the others jeered, her mother ignored them and would whisper down to Cresella that normal or not, she was a witch and was deserving.

The smell of baking cookies mixed with her tree hollow's damp wood and hanging bags of toad's wart, leechlily, dragon's bane, winterdrops, snappers, and fairy wings. She ducked around one of the bags, head bent as she came closer to the stove, checking to make sure the fires burning below were at just the right height. Too low and the gingerbread men would come out malformed and gooey. No one wanted melted gingerbread that tried to move and couldn't. Too high, well, no one with a body stiffer than steel—not even a magical cookie—could move then.

From outside came the unmistakable crunch of snow and leaves that only an early snow could produce. The frost and steam covering her windows blocked the outside world. Only light was able to pass through, and even that was faint.

A knock came at the door; it echoed like a bell in her small hollow.

Cresella grimaced before fixing her face into something more pleasant. The humans always wanted nice-looking, warm and gentle and wonderful. At least, that was true for her business. How she envied the witches who could scowl and get paid for it.

She hopped up and swept over to the door, letting a pleasant little smile wrap up her lips. "Hello, welcome to Cresella's Cookies and Fineries, come on in." She cringed at the name.

The man waiting outside was young, somewhere between graduating from college and being settled in life. Snow rested on his golden hair and broad shoulders. A scarf wrapped around his neck, pushing up toward cheeks flushed with cold. He smiled, waved before pulling his hand back down and looking away.

"Hi…uhhh…Cresella, right?"

She nodded and stepped back, letting the man duck into her home. He straightened, almost banging his head into a pot that hung just off the doorway. Her eyes widened. She'd never noticed that pot there. Have to move it before she lost a client or two from a concussion.

"That would be me." She lifted a finger, one far too pinkish and smooth, before pulling her hand back down and stuffing it in her black robes. "I take it you'd like gingerbread men? They do a lovely job of running around and talking nonstop about how they can't be caught."

He turned his head to the side. "Can they be caught?"

"Of course they can." She paused. Mostly, but no need to scare clients with the stories of gingerbread men who escaped and lived in the vents for a few years. "When you think about it practically, they are tiny and have little legs. Oh, sure, they like to go on about how they can't be caught, but that's just the show of it." She nodded along with her story. "You have to *pretend* they're fast, and when you do catch them, I recommend not eating the feet. They get…let's say dirty. That's a nice way to put it."

"Oh."

He seemed taken aback and glanced at the door, now closed behind him. The man looked as though he realized where he truly was, his cheeks sucking in and breaths coming out faster. That was how it was with so many humans. Coming out of their world seemed so wonderful until they crossed the divide between the human world and the Thicket Beyond, stepping into a whole different dimension altogether. Then reality hit. A reality with all the magic and wonders…and horrors.

The man's gaze settled on Bruno, and he edged a step back. "Uhh, well, I'm sorry, see, I didn't, well, didn't come for gingerbread men, though I heard yours are the best around! I was… Do you, uhh, happen to make snowballs?"

Cresella had, unfortunately, become very well acquainted with all the different types of cookies and Christmastime goodies. She nodded, trying to hold in a sigh. "Would you like snowballs that are cold to the touch or the ones that make snow fall on them or both?"

"I'm not really interested in the snow part."

"That is what a snowball does. It snows."

She cleared her throat, reminding herself to keep her voice in line. A client, however dumb and good-looking, was still a client. She paused for a moment, wondering why in the devil's browned earth she would ever think the man was good-looking. Well, he was good-looking for human standards, but…but that wasn't the point. Even after a few hundred years of the Thicket Beyond and human world interacting, the inhabitants of both worlds never really meshed well. A human and a witch being together, even the idea of a couple like that was just silly.

She shivered as the thought of humans and witches mingling retreated, and she forced up another smile, wider than any of the others. "Then maybe a different kind of cookie would be best. Why don't you tell me what you're looking for?"

His hand wove through his blond locks, and a smile began to poke at his lips, the nervous hitches of skin pricking up and falling back down. "Ahhh, yes, well. Maybe this isn't the right season…but…do you make cookies that…well…that make someone love you?"

Of course. The age-old hunt for love. Valentine's

Day was the typical time of the year when the humans would be swarming into the Thicket Beyond, specifically the Hollows, where the witches lived, looking for love potions. Every year, Cresella was just so sure the humans would've learned by now love potions didn't make people fall in love. But no. Every Valentine's Day— every single one—they'd step past the divide, their heads buried in their little smartphones, and then glance up at the thick, old trees in the Hollows. And they'd come, asking Cresella, asking any witch they could, if there was a potion, a spell, something to make a secret desire love them.

She held back a sharp word or two trying to edge past her lips, her smile beginning to crack like old porcelain. "Love doesn't work that way. All I can do, *any* of us can do, is make an aphrodisiac. At best, your potential lover will be more…aware of you. But love doesn't work in potions and enchantments. Love is its own spell."

"Then which cookie can do that?"

"Be an aphrodisiac?"

"Yes, exactly, make someone…well, notice me more, right?"

She nodded, slowly, measuring him. "Odd request during the holidays, but love is love, and we all have our reasons. I'd say the best cookie that'll do the trick and still be fitting with the season would be a peppermint snap. They can be romantic…in their own sort of way."

He nodded all too eagerly. The snow had now melted into his hair, whipping off in droplets of water. "Great! Yes, I'll have that. And can I have some gingerbread men, too? They sound like fun."

"Bushels of fun." She couldn't keep the sarcasm from dripping through every word.

He fiddled with his hands. "Uhh, you know, maybe you don't remember, but I was… You know, a few times before, I've ordered from you."

Now that he mentioned it, the man *did* look familiar, but she had a habit of not remembering her customers by name. It was the proper witch thing to do, actually. The more inhuman the witches acted, the more their clients ate it up. Not that she tried for the whole act in *her* line of business, but it gave a great excuse for a weak memory and attitude to match.

"Lot of humans come through here." She waved her hand, standing up and sliding over to her oven. "Nothing personal."

"Course, right." He bit at his lip and shifted his weight from one foot to the other, enough to draw Bruno's attention and make the basilisk shift from leg to leg as though getting ready to play a game of catch the dragon scale.

Cresella glanced over her shoulder at the man. "You do realize it takes time to bake cookies?"

"Oh, yes, of course." He stepped back, almost tripping on the rug, and regained some composure before banging his head on the pot. The man crumbled to his knees and groaned, and without thinking, she flew to his side and placed a hand on his arm.

"Are you all right?" The concern that came out surprised her. Even more surprising was how close she was to him, her face inches from his. His cologne was soft, nothing striking or over the top like most men wore. Definitely better than that garbage fish-oil stuff the satyrs put on.

Rubbing his head, he turned, blushed a deep red, and scrambled to his feet. "Oh, yes, fine. Thank you." He reached the door, fumbled with the overly large knob.

She shook away the flutters inside her, those silly little things that spoke of feelings. For a human? First a satyr and now a human? She was probably just delirious from not eating enough today. When was the last time she ate? Breakfast?

"Name!" she blurted out before glancing away. She cleared her throat. "For the order. What name should I put it under?"

Halfway out the door, he paused and looked back in. "Oh, dear, that's right." He smiled, so flashingly bright she could melt. "Walter. My name is Walter Hindsdale. And…oh, well, I have more questions if you didn't mind."

"More cookies?"

"Not quite. I was curious if…if you happen to deliver."

"Home deliveries? That costs extra. Quite a bit considering the distance." The distance actually wasn't that far, but she liked to make these things seem difficult.

"That's fine. I'd be more than happy to pay. You see, I have a party tomorrow evening. A holiday get-together with friends, and I'll be too busy to come and take them. I'd love for you to stop over—stop by." He cleared his throat. "I live in Notting Hill, 13 Chestshire Way."

"Yes, I'll bring the cookies." Cresella waved Walter off. "Good evening." She closed the door on him and turned to go back to the stove.

"Love during the holidays," she mumbled to herself. "The poor thing must watch too many of those Christmas movies."

Bruno glanced up from his spot at the foot of the bed, and his tongue licked the air.

She pushed a finger at him. "Don't you start. I can take pity on humans, can't I? They are dumb in so many ways."

He glared back at her.

Her eyes narrowed. "Don't you dare suggest that either. Humans can be good-looking, too. And it's not like it would be forbidden. Humans and the fae creatures have been together before." She threw up her hands. "Why am I *having* this conversation with you in the first place? Keep it up, and I'll kick you out in the snow. Then you'll *really* be cold-blooded."

He pushed a puff of air out of his nostrils.

"No, Bruno, he did not ask me to come to the party. I'm delivering the cookies. He said…" Her eyes widened. "Did he really?"

He nodded.

"I should call this off, then. I can't…with a *human*. Even if he is…" She found herself pacing in a flurry of small circles. She threw up her hands. "But he's a client. I should at least drop off the cookies, right?"

He rolled his eyes.

"Oh, you are just the worst familiar. What would you have me do, then, hmm?" She crossed her arms.

He turned his head to the side.

"No, I'm not trying Kettle and Cauldron again. It keeps matching me with orcs looking to have fun." She shook her head, going to the stove and pulling out the gingerbread men. "I'll just drop off the cookies. That's all."

****

Stepping out of—or into, depending on which direction one was headed—the Thicket Beyond was a lesson in short-term, *very* short-term, G-force training.

The silvery air that hung around the edges of the Thicket Beyond was deceivingly beautiful, with glimmers and sparks that caught the hints of light from the Hollows behind. The air hummed with the power of the barrier between the two worlds, a soft song barely resting on lips before being brought to life. If one were to look out from the Hollows, it would seem as though the lands beyond the divide kept rolling away forever, with green hills and distant forests that showed no hint of the Thicket Beyond coming to an end and the human world being only a step away.

Sometimes, Cresella wished she could see the human world from within the Thicket, but this would be quite confusing. Depending on what one thought about as they crossed the divide, stepping out of the Thicket could lead to any place in the world one wished. The Thicket Beyond was not so tidy as the human world, more a warped sphere encasing every inch of the human's dimension. She could hardly imagine *that* view.

A quick left step, then right, and a thought about London, and she was through. The silver glimmer of the divide crushed her like a tin can under a press, the quick slap of weight almost dropping her to her knees before vanishing as fast it came. She sucked in the thick air. The fumes of cars and tastes of firewood burned.

She shivered and pulled her black cloak around herself. The pedestrians moving along the streets only briefly glanced her way—seeing someone pop out of thin air was so normal that it had become as common as a taxi going past. She shook the snow off her cloak and moved away from the brightly colored light-blue building she had appeared next to, mingling in with the people carrying their shopping bags and so full of their holiday glee.

Notting Hill was a unique part of London, a bit farther out, though Cresella couldn't say she knew that much about London—or any other part of the human world for that matter. She did, though, like the ways the buildings were painted, a bright pink squeezed next to a faded yellow pressed next to a light green. Most of the witches in the Hollows would prefer the bland grays and muted browns of stone, would probably prefer even darker colors. Blacks and grays and dim and dark, that's the witch's way.

When she turned a corner, she paused, stepping off to the side as a family, bundled to the eyes and brimming with their holiday spirits in their sing-songy conversations, skipped along. They passed in smiles and glee, and it was—Cresella had to admit—infectious. In the good kind of way.

She turned onto Chestshire Way and scanned each number, eventually coming to 13. Well, that was a nice number.

The terrace was like all the others pressed together, so cramped unlike the Hollows' trees with space and more between. Standing on the sidewalk, the light peeking out from behind closed curtains, she looked at the door, then at her dress and back again. Without her usual witch robes, she was without her armor, without the thing that brought her into the folds of the witch community. She rubbed her fingers together, the basket hanging on her arm swinging.

Bruno had laughed his scaly head off about Cresella deciding to dress like a human, leaving her pointed hat behind and just taking the cloak. She felt silly and ridiculous. Just outright wrong dressed so much like a human woman. What *was* she trying to do?

She couldn't remember walking up the steps or lifting the golden ring under the numbers thirteen. The knocker hitting the door with a gentle thud swept her out of her daze, and she glanced over her shoulder and thought about running. She could do it. Leave the basket like some abandoned child and be gone, safe and back home and done with this business—whatever it was—she was doing.

The door swung open. A gush of warm air billowed out.

"Oh!" Walter stuttered and stepped back. "It's you! I mean…" He cleared his throat. "Yes, well, hello. Do come in."

"Oh, thank you." Her eyes were unable to look into his. She found it much more comforting to stare beyond him into his kitchen where a bowl of popcorn lay half dug into on the island, crowded by regular cookies and chips and a platter of cheeses and crackers. "I really don't know if I can stay. I just brought the batch to drop off, that's all."

"Please, you came all this way. At least warm up. It's getting chilly out." He waved his hand like a mad air traffic controller until she stepped in and shut the door behind.

"Really, I'll just be a minute."

Inside, the warmth of a fireplace crackling and the closeness of people pressed in. Smells of popcorn freshly popped and buttered, deep aromas of wine and bourbon hung in the air like old guests who hadn't left the last party. A small group passed by the entrance, went up the stairs to join in the plods of steps above.

The vibrancy, the very vibe of laughter and cheer and

so many bundled together so tightly, settled over Cresella in prickling unease. She glanced around like a transfer coming into a new school. Her home was tiny, a tree hollow like all the other witches', and the most excitement she ever had was when a gingerbread man escaped. Otherwise, it was quiet. Just the routine of another day, another batch to bake.

Walter eased her cloak off and hung it up with the guests' coats, where it stuck out as plainly as, well, she did. She brought the basket closer to her, hugging her arms.

"I can get you a drink," Walter said with a smile. "Why don't you come have a look? I tried to get a good selection."

She nodded and followed him down the hall to the kitchen where people leaned on the island and a light banter fought with "Santa Baby."

Walter reached under the island and brought up a couple bottles of wine. "Want to start with the reds or the whites?"

Her wine tastes consisted of mostly Frog Berry Reds. Frog berries were one of the better berries that grew on the backs of amphibians, and in wines, well, they packed a punch. She pointed to a bottle of red wine with a horse rearing up on the label. "That one looks fine, but really, don't worry about me. I can't stay long."

"Is...is something wrong?" He fumbled with the wine glasses. One slipped from his fingers and shattered.

The group nearby stopped and turned, and Walter met their stares with a shrug and smile. They rolled their eyes, as if to say they knew this would happen, as if to show how well they knew Walter compared with her. The new girl. A pang of jealousy worked through her, and she grabbed her hands together and wrung them, wondering where *that* had come from.

"Let me help." She was next to him, picking up the shards.

"I'm so sorry. I always end up being such a butterfingers."

She smiled. "We call it frog-slimed palms."

"Is frog slime that slippery?" he asked with a laugh.

"Worse than oil." She rolled her eyes and joined in laughing with him.

When she plucked one of the last shards from the floor, she glanced up and noticed just how close he was to her. Her heart winged around in her chest like a bat with earmuffs on, and she turned her head, hoping her face wasn't ten shades redder than normal. For once, she was thrilled she didn't have green skin. Even the slightest of red showed up on those witches' faces.

Walter reached out for a shard close to her, his hand glancing against hers. His face went wide and blank. His eyes trembled as if locked in place and wanting to look anywhere but Cresella.

She grabbed the glass, rubbing against his hand, letting her fingers linger. The touch was too good. The warmth too nice. Human or not, she didn't care, and she couldn't lie to herself anymore about why she'd come, about what she thought of Walter, about any of it.

"I got it," she said in a soft voice. "I—"

"Walt!" A man dressed in a crimson sweater, stitched so horribly it looked to be straight off a lamb, clapped Walter on the back. He smiled so wide Cresella was sure it had to hurt, that surely the ebony-colored cheeks would crack at some point. She rubbed her face as she stood up.

"Luther!" Walter brought the man in for a hug.

"Sorry again to run off today and leave you with that mess in the office."

He shrugged. "Wasn't that bad. The holidays tend to make people a little less…aggressive. All good." His gaze stumbled on Cresella. "So sorry, didn't realize you two were—"

"We weren't." She held up the pieces of the wine glass. "I was just helping clean up."

"This guy. Sometimes, I swear he's cursed."

Walter spun and looked at Luther. "Uhh, I…well, that sort of language."

She waved Walter off. "We don't actually do curses. That's a sorcerer sort of thing."

Luther glanced around. "Is there…something… I'm sorry, what's going on?"

Walter took in a deep breath. "This is Cresella. She's…a witch. From the Thicket Beyond."

That look of knowing, a final piece of some long-played-out puzzle finally falling into place. Luther slowly nodded. "A witch." He grinned like a troll in an alehouse. "Yeah, the witch. I've heard a lot about you, Cresella."

"You have?"

Walter cleared his throat. "All right then, enough of the introductions. We are, you know, at a party of sorts. Why don't we act like it?" He wiggled about. "And, you know, get down with it."

Cresella slapped a hand over her mouth to stop herself from laughing.

"Oh, Walt. No one's said that in ages." Luther stepped back. "Was nice meeting you, Cresella. We'll catch up later,"

She had never minded the silence in her hollow. The quiet of oak finding a way to compress the soft huff of flames and crackling wood and the wind as it rattled the tree.

She couldn't say she liked this silence, even though the kitchen was anything but quiet, with people talking and music playing, glasses chiming and plates being scraped clean of baked clams and scalloped shrimp. She wound her hands in her dress.

"Well—"

"Uhh—"

"Sorry," she and Walter said together, turning their heads when they did.

He let out a long breath. "I'm sorry about all of that."

"He's nice. There's nothing to be sorry about."

"He can be a bit…straight to the point. And, you know, I didn't mention you all *that* much to him. Not truly." He poured a glass of red wine and set it on the island next to her. "I mean, we talk. About everything. We were friends in college, coworkers now if you can believe it. Same job, same place. Always like that—on the same wavelength."

"Right, but you were talking about me?" Her head began to spin without her taking a sip of the wine. "About inviting me to your party?"

He nodded. "Yes! Exactly that. That's all. Just telling him about your cookies, first, and then how it'd be nice to have you over to the party."

She stared into his green eyes. "Why *did* you invite me?" Turning from him, she tried to find strength in the red wine and gulped down half of it in one go. Her hands shook. Her legs could've been a baby goat's. "I'm not the sort of person—if you can call me that—people would want to have over."

From the kitchen, she could peer into the living

room, lit only by the fireplace. A group of young women, tight dresses, lips red and plump, bodies a model would be jealous of, hung around the fireplace, drinking and whispering and laughing.

"See? Look at them."

"Who?" he asked, coming over to stand next to her.

"Those women. They are gorgeous, by human standards, of course."

"Witches have different standards?"

"Have you seen a real witch?"

He shrugged. "I'm looking at one."

"Not me." She sighed. "A *normal* witch."

"True, you're not normal. Better than normal, I'd say."

She gulped. "That's not the point. See, those women—they are better, in every way. Why even invite me? Am I the show for tonight?"

He grabbed her free hand and turned her gently so she was facing him. "I—well, how do I say this?" He cleared his throat and cast his gaze down. "See, for a while now, I've...I've fancied you. Think you are amazing and kind."

"Witches aren't supposed to be kind."

His head came up, tilted to the side. "It's not a bad thing, you know. I like people who are kind. The world has enough wankers. We could use a few more of the good ones like you."

He leaned in, eyes closing, and she couldn't resist. Didn't want to resist. She moved in closer. His breath brushed against her in soft strokes, cinnamon and mint and wine all mingled together, and she wanted nothing more than to taste that. To taste him.

"Let's get the games going!" a voice called out.

168

Walter pulled back before he could kiss her and smiled so sadly, so sweetly, that she wanted to run a hand through his hair and tell him it was all right.

She bit her lip and nodded to the commotion in the living room. "It is your party, after all. The host should be around."

"Right, well, off to my duties." He hadn't let go of her hand and pulled her along. "Come on, it'll be great."

The twenty or thirty guests—Cresella couldn't quite count the number, but it felt like a lot, far too many for her tastes—squeezed into the living room. She knew of human games, of course. Everyone in the Thicket Beyond *knew* of them. But she'd never quite understood what they'd meant or how to play.

First came charades. She would've preferred to sit out, but Walter took her hand and said he had his partner. Some looks came, mostly from the other women, but Cresella ignored them as best she could and focused on the game…which was hard. How someone was supposed to infer words from half-drunken movements was beyond her. Needless to say, Walter and Cresella did not do so well in charades. If only they had played unicorn horseshoes.

Next was a drinking game, a very drawn-out game of "I never." Being a witch at a human party made Cresella have to take a sip almost every time. They might as well have stuck a cat in her place and asked it if it'd ever kissed on top of a Ferris wheel or worked overtime and lied about it. Though, the last one was rather unfair to all the self-employed who might have been there.

Afterward, much to Cresella's embarrassment, they played catch the gingerbread man. The little bugger went on and on about how it couldn't be caught and hopped off people's legs and underneath the couch and then back around near the window, where it stopped and stuck out a vanilla-frosted tongue. Eventually, they did catch it, at the expense of two vases and a picture frame. And the winner, a short man named Greg, stuffed it all down in one gulp. Even the legs.

By the time the games wound down and the music turned from Christmas to pop, Cresella was feeling the effects of the wine. A sway here and almost bumping into an end table there. Just a nice feeling overall. Lightness, as though the world had forgotten to hound her for a minute. It even gave her the courage—or maybe just the lack of presence of mind—to talk to other people.

With the fire burning low, on its last bits of log, only a few guests remained, and Cresella began to realize in the painful sharpness of a clearing fog broken by the sunlight that she'd overstayed her welcome. She found Walter upstairs, poking through his closet and pulling out a small bundle of gifts for the guests about to leave.

"I should get going, too," she said in a near whisper. "It's been…nice, though, thank you."

With an armful of red and green wrapped gifts, he turned and blinked as though lost. "Leaving? So soon?"

"It's…it's late," she said at last.

His eyes had a haze to them, and a few moments passed before he nodded. "Oh, right, well. Hold on. Just a quick moment. Let me find your gift."

He dropped the gifts in his arms. She cringed, expecting a crash of glass or crunch of something metallic, but they landed with tiny puffs as though pillows letting out air. He burrowed through his closet. Out came a sweater. Then a tennis racket.

"You really don't need to give me anything." She

ducked in time to dodge a cricket bat.

"Nonsense, everyone at the party gets a gift. Now, I know I put yours in the back here. Just…well, this is embarrassing." A pair of pants launched over his head. "Ah. Here we are." He came out with a small box wrapped in silver paper, a red bow on top.

"Th-thank you." She hoped the red in her cheeks wasn't too bright. "I…I really should go, though."

"I can walk you home if you'd like."

She laughed. "Once we get into the Thicket, I'd be the one escorting you."

He laughed with her. "True. What a place that is. I love it there."

"You do?"

"Of course. Who doesn't love wonder?"

"Most people…and most witches, for that matter." She stepped back, bit her lip. "It was nice, tonight. Thank you."

"W-wait!" He reached out and grabbed her hand. "I'd rather not have to buy cookies each time I see you." His eyes went wide enough to become tea saucers. "Not that I don't love your cookies. In fact, I love them too much. I'll become a snowball myself if I keep eating them. I just meant…well, I was hoping I could see you another time."

If he hadn't been holding her hand, she might've stumbled back and fumbled her way down the stairs, kept going until she passed out. A date. He wanted to go out on a date with *her*? She shouldn't. Witches and humans had a horrible history together. Yet tonight…tonight had been nothing short of magical. And that was coming from someone with a bit of magic.

"Tomorrow night all right?" she asked, the words

slipping out before she could stop herself.

"I'll pick you up."

"A date in the Hollows?" Her eyebrows perked up. "Aren't *you* adventurous!"

"Luther would never believe it."

"The having a date in the Hollows part or having a date?" she asked with a grin.

Walter only smiled and nodded.

****

Cresella had spent the day baking a massive hoard of cookies for no particular reason at all. Ever since she'd been a little witch living in the nook of an apple tree not far down the path, she'd baked whenever she was upset or nervous or just not feeling herself. Today, she was all of those things wrapped up in her very own Christmas package.

As the twilight cast a luster of purple and pink over her floors, she sat in her rocking chair, a small silver locket in her hand. To say she'd been surprised to find a locket in Walter's gift would be an understatement. Had everyone gotten a gift like that? The answer was too obvious, and it twisted her stomach into a sourdough knot.

There was nothing horrible about such a lovely gift. Despite her having nothing for him in exchange. No, it was the idea of getting a gift, of the thought of something nice being more like a bribe. Which led her down a path too familiar, too much like…oh, she even hated the thing's name. Helios. Her oh-so-lovely, cheating ex.

Bruno worked his way out from under her bed and glanced at her.

She turned her head. "Done up? What's that supposed to mean?"

Basilisks didn't have the shoulders for shrugging, but he tried his best.

"You're telling me I look *too* good. What was I supposed to do? Roll around in the mud and snow and stick some twigs in my hair?"

He seemed to nod.

"You don't like him, do you?"

He held her gaze.

"Oh, because he's human, is that what you're telling me? Well, I…I don't care. He's nice. And it's not like the other witches have ever been kind to me. I don't know, I just…I just fit with him."

Basilisks had trouble looking anything other than, well, a basilisk, but he had adopted disappointment to the point he could have taught an acting class on it.

"Well *that* was a long tirade. Lovely, Bruno. I appreciate the effort. But you don't see why he's different. You don't get that maybe, just maybe, I need to stop caring about what everyone thinks and find someone *I* like."

Although she did care. Always had. Never had Cresella been able to find a hollow or nook just right, wiggle and worm her way into a business, a witchery pursuit that would fit her. She'd always felt one wheel short of a wagon, and the other witches had made that clear. Even Helios had been an attempt to fit in. A poor, stupid attempt.

But with Walter, things were different. She could almost picture a life in London with him. Maybe even in the Hollows. Imagine the uproar that would cause. She grinned at the thought and ran a hand through her straightened black hair, whisking a strand behind her ear.

She snapped out of it. "What did you say, Bruno?"

Her familiar stepped back, head down.

"Daydreaming and in love? You're *ridiculous*." She stood up and hovered over the basilisk before bending down and rubbing under his chin. "But you'll always be my familiar. Is that what you're worried about?"

He turned his head away.

"And you're worried about me? Well, I didn't think basilisks were supposed to be kind. I suppose that's why you're my familiar. We odd muffins should stick together."

He glanced around their hollow.

"Oh, worried about the business, too? Then consider this a business date. Maybe if Walter and I hit it off, he'd recommend me to friends. Word supposedly spreads fast with humans."

He rolled his eyes.

"Oh, fine, so it's not a business date. And, really, it's more just friends getting together."

He lifted a paw.

"I can wear a nice dress if I want to. And another thing—"

A knock came at the door, and she bolted up straight, the locket gripped in her palm. Her arms went out like a bird about to take off, and she spun and inspected every inch of her home. She'd cleaned but…but was it good enough? She swallowed. Pitter-patters like tiny feet warbled along her throat and down to her chest, and there, they turned into thumps so strong she was afraid lifting up a foot would send her off-balance.

Another knock. She let out a breath and went to the door.

"Hi," Walter said, the biggest, dumbest grin she'd ever seen on a soul plastered on his face. "Do you need a minute?"

She shook her head a bit too fast. "No. Of course not. I'm…I'm all set." She held up the silver locket. "But do you think you can help put this on?"

She turned and brushed her hair over one shoulder. His fingers were slightly cool. The wind from outside trailed across her skin, prickling her flesh into goose bumps. She shivered with his touch, warm now, and held her breath as he fiddled with the lock and clasp.

"All set," he said softly.

She turned to see a face red enough to make an apple look pale, and she was sure they were a matching pair.

Closing the door, she whispered to Bruno, "And you be good."

****

The silence between them settled like a sand burr caught in a sock. Unpleasant, jabbing at times, and all too difficult to remove.

With her arm folded into his, they walked along the snow-packed lanes. Lanterns hung from twisted oak staffs, the pale yellow of the light barely enough to see by. Every tree they passed brimmed with light, though, sometimes with the movement of a witch or two inside. Once, even, Cresella saw a green nose pressed against the glass.

Only after passing by Matilda's Brooms and Things did she realize where they were going. Walter was, of course, taking the long way to what had to be the Toad and Onion, a restaurant set at the edge of the Hollows near the border between the Thicket Beyond and the human world. Much of the Hollows—even large parts of the civilized areas in the Thicket Beyond—had turned into tourist traps over the years. Chief among them was the

Toad and Onion, where humans could pop in for a bite to eat and have just a hint of the mystical. More like eating at a human fast-food restaurant in Italy or France and claiming to have eaten the local food.

They were halfway down a hill draped by snow-coated willow branches, where the light played like fireflies and specks of fairy dust trailed in the air, when Walter cleared his throat and said, "I…I wasn't sure if you'd, well, you know, like the gift."

Cresella touched the silver locket. Smooth and cold, and for a second, her fingers lingered there. "I don't know what to say. Did everyone get something so nice?"

"If you enjoy Christmas-themed dishtowels, then, yes, everyone did."

She giggled and turned her head. "You…" She licked her lips, finding the words hard to come by. "You didn't have to. Shouldn't have." She stopped and waited until he turned. "You barely know me!"

"True, but I'd like to know a lot more."

"Is that what this is? A bribe?" She wanted to grin, but again, her stomach twisted and turned at the thought of all the little tokens Helios had tossed her way.

"I like to think of it more like a gesture of my appreciation." He took her hand.

They walked a few steps, the crunch of snow underneath their feet and the air thick with fairy dust. Swirls of pink and orange and purple and blue hung like paint that forgot gravity. Cresella eyed a fairy hiding in the branch of a maple. A tiny tongue appeared, fingers wiggling by its ear. Such wild little things.

"I appreciate the appreciation," she said. "It's not a common thing around here."

"No?"

"Witches are, well, quite different from humans. The real witches, that is."

He squeezed her hand. "You *are* a real one."

She rolled her eyes. "Tell that to the other witches and see what happens."

A blanket of lights sitting just outside the Hollows rose up from the snow. Even though the food might cater to tourists, she appreciated the building itself, a toadstool large enough to fit any ten trees in the Hollows inside. Windows had been cut out of the sides, and pockets of light shone a few stories up.

"This is something, isn't it?" He glanced at her. "Okay, maybe not for you. Did I pick a good spot?" His face glowed a deep red. "I just didn't know what else to do, and when I did research on the Thicket Beyond, well, this—"

She lifted the locket. "You picked really well."

A burly orc with arms bigger than most branches led them to a table on the third story where they could sit and look over the Christmas tree rising in the center, all the way to the top of the toadstool. It made the humans happy, Cresella was sure, but even she thought it was nice. A little human mixed into the Thicket had a certain charm.

"Look at this menu." As Walter flipped through the plastic-coated pages, the stick-and-Velcro-sound released with each turn. "The wine selection alone is four pages."

She leaned forward, dropping her voice. "You've never been here before?"

He glanced over the menu. "Well, no, I thought it'd be nice to try for the first time. Experience something new and all. Have you?"

"I've never had the occasion."

"If we had our wine, I'd say we should toast to that,

but at this rate, I'll have our wine picked out just in time to ring in the New Year."

She smiled. "Need help?"

"No, never. Though if you have any suggestions…"

She picked up the menu and scanned over it. He was right about there being far too many choices. As she came to page two of the red wines, she heard the snicker and giggles a few tables down. She peered around the menu to find a table of witches sitting in a booth near a window. The lantern hung low, washing a yellow light over their green skin. When she locked eyes with one, a grin appeared on the witch's face. Knowing. Cruel.

"How about the pinot? Or are you feeling more in the mood for a white?"

She turned her head from the witches, a sudden pang rushing through her. A realization that maybe this could never work out. No matter how nice Walter was, no matter how badly they wanted to make it happen between them. Some worlds should never be brought together. Some lives were too far apart to find common ground.

"Red's fine," she said softly.

"Everything all right? Did the read through the wine list tire you out?" He chuckled. "I'm about ready to pass out myself. We can order an appetizer with the wine. Is the fairy-dust-seared deathworm any good?"

"Walter…" She let out a sigh. "Why did you want to go out with me?"

He placed down the menu and folded his hands over it. "That's easy."

"Is it? Walter, we're…we're nothing alike."

"I wouldn't say that." He leaned back in his chair and looked up at the lanterns hanging from the ceiling, the vines looping from one to the next. "My father would tell me that no matter how different people are, they're all the same. Which I thought was rubbish at the time. I could never know what someone else is going through, someone who didn't grow up with a nice family like me or who had to wonder where the next meal was coming from, if it was coming at all.

"But I began to realize he was right. Actually, it was with Luther, in college. It kinda hit me then, when we were both studying for a final on economics, I could see how stressed he was. Same as me. Switch our spots, and it'd be the same nervous, overstressed guy there. It didn't matter he'd grown up in Liverpool and me London. Didn't matter he has three siblings and I have none. Underneath it all, we all feel the same. Just, maybe, in different ways."

"Yes, but say this"—she waved a hand between them—"works out. What then? Do you come to live in the Thicket Beyond? Do I live in London? How would that even work?"

"Do they say the devil is in the details over here?"

"No, but I rather like that."

He grinned. "You're overthinking everything, Cresella." He reached out a hand and took hers. "If things are meant to be, they're meant to be."

"Oh, let me guess, you grew up watching those silly romantic comedies."

He turned his head. "They're not silly. They're hopeful."

"Which one?"

He turned to look at her. "Which one what?"

"Is your favorite? You seem a *Love Actually* kind of person."

His eyes lit up. "So you like them, too!"

"I've watched…a few. Or at least I used to. Those and fairy tales. Fairy tales are big in the Thicket Beyond. Imagine that."

He laughed. "We should watch *Enchanted*, then. It's the best of both worlds."

She ran her finger over his hand. "I think I like the best of both worlds. And, by the way, deathworm is chewy. Good, but more like jerky than anything else. I'd go for the—"

She heard the hooves a moment before smelling the cologne thick enough a goblin would drown. The giggling from the witches turned into a full-out brew-ha-ha, and they kept on going, even with Cresella looking at them.

Helios was a satyr much like any other: the bottom half a goat, the top a man, horns poking out from the head, and a beard because like any overly manly man, he needed a beard. He wore a shortened pair of dress pants, a white button-down shirt almost all the way open, and tweed jacket that fell somewhere between professor wannabe and boy trying to look cool. The hair around his curled horns was slicked back and thick with grease, and a single flower poked out from the top of his ear.

He swooped over to her, pulled out the flower, and grinned with a pearly white smile. "There you are, my love. I was told I could find you here."

She rolled her eyes and slapped the flower from his hand. "Get that thing away from me."

"Love?" Walter slipped his hand out from hers. "I-I thought you were single. Is this your…uhh…husband? Or boyfriend? No, wait, partner, yes, sorry. That would be the word."

Helios wrapped an arm around her. "Yes, it is true.

She is my lover. We are the spring rabbits who cannot stop."

She pushed him away, slapping his cheek as she did. "*Never* were we spring rabbits. And *you cheated on me*." She sighed and looked at Walter. "What a lovely date this has turned out to be. Walter, meet my *ex*, Helios."

"Ah, yes, about that so-called cheating. It was a one-time mistake. The worst in my life."

"*Twice*."

Helios's gaze jumped around. "A horrible, awful, double mistake. Such things happen, but never again." He grabbed her hand and planted kisses on the back of it. "On my word."

She yanked away. "How many women have you said that to today?"

He placed a hand over his heart. "You hurt me, my love. Never would I make such promises to anyone but you!"

"So if I can ask—" Walter began.

She whipped her head around. "Not now, please."

He nodded, but how broken he seemed. The little child finding his gifts on Christmas morning, now the man coming down to find a tree empty, a house with nothing but cold, and a fire waiting to be started. The magic gone.

"I promise, my love." Helios fawned. "I will never hurt you."

"Cut the toad stool, Helios. I don't want to see you, and I don't give the devil's ass what you want." She crossed her arms. "Could you please leave us alone now?"

He straightened and played with his vest. "Ah, if only I could. Even though I truly did wish to reunite with my one true love, I come on business."

"Business?" She was beginning to suspect what kind of business he would come to her about. Only a few traders ran to the Hollows. Helios, unfortunately, was one of them.

He grinned. "Do you remember saying you would do anything for yeti tears?"

She trembled, eyes growing large. "You don't mean…"

"I've found a way, my love. Unfrozen, at that."

Walter looked from one of them to the other. "Yeti tears?"

She swallowed, voice cracking. "Yetis are rare in the Thicket Beyond. And when most people find them, they either run off or rip you limb from limb. Immune to magic, thick furred and skinned. They're…what do you call those metal things you humans fight in?"

"Tanks?"

"Yes, that, but much worse. If the trick was just getting yeti fur or bone, that would be a challenge in and of itself. But yetis don't cry. Ever."

Helios pulled a chair from a nearby table and scooted close to Cresella. "And if they did, up in the mountains, the tears would be frozen in a flash." He snapped his fingers. "Just like that. Useless things, then. But I've found a way."

She folded her arms. "You're lying."

"Oh, then I can go to Brunhilda or Maive or—"

"What is it you want?"

"Nothing."

She belted out a laugh. "Yeti tears for free? No one would be that dumb." Though Helios was not the brightest satyr this side of the Thicket. Clever, maybe. A good businesscreature, no doubt. And that made her worry.

"I want to make, shall we say, an agreement." He raised a finger. "I can't get the yeti tears alone. I need a witch for the job. Come with me, work with me on this, my love, and we'll split the profit. Fair enough?"

"A partnership?"

He grabbed her hand. "More, I would hope."

She recoiled. "Never."

"Just business, then?" he asked with a grin.

She sat a moment, eyes closed. With the profits from even one tear, she could open a shop in the human world, branch out her business, really *be* something. How she'd love to stick it to those other witches and laugh in their faces for once. "Fine. When do we leave?"

"Tonight." Helios stood up. "From Gretchen's Inn and Hearth."

As Helios was walking away, Walter cleared his throat and said, "Wonderful, we'll see you there."

"We?" Cresella asked.

He shrugged. "I've always wanted to see the mountains. And the Alps just don't cut it."

****

At the other end of the Hollows lay a tangle of large willows, branches intertwined and weeping fronds so tangled they became a sheet of green laced with clinging snow. Wagons sat alongside the narrow dirt road leading up to the willows, almost blocking the sign that read *Gretchen's Inn and Hearth*.

With Walter in tow, Cresella stopped next to a familiar-looking yellow-painted wagon and leaned against the aged wood. She hated the thing and the memories that came with it. Specifically the one where she thought how odd it was the wagon was rocking on its own, only to find Helios and Matilda in the back. What a lovely evening *that* had turned out to be.

For a moment, the ground felt a bit heavier, the world spinning a bit slower. It was tiring thinking of Helios, of trying to save her business, of that silly thing called hope she had with Walter. Sometimes, it was all too much.

Walter shifted next to her, his backpack shuffling with the sounds of crudely packed clothes and necessities jumbling against each other. "It's starting to get dark."

She stared out past the Hollows, out to the Razerthorn Mountains beyond. Vines thicker than trees dug into the stone, sharp with thorns that bled red in the dying sun's light. "That's generally how days go. They eventually turn to night."

He chuckled softly, nervously. "Oh, yes, no, I mean are we going to rest here for the night and leave in the morning?"

Truly, it would've been smart. Helios, though, was not a smart satyr. She whipped her hand around and began to walk toward the inn. "Some fae enjoy the night." Though she didn't want to mention that a good number of fae creatures enjoyed the night too much and that coming across such creatures would not bode well for their journey. She turned to him. "You can always go back. Why don't you? This isn't safe."

He shrugged. "I suppose it isn't."

"I'm sorry about this whole mess. On our first date, too."

"Well, it is...odd, but this whole venture with the yetis seems important."

They pushed inside the inn where a film of dark coated the willow wood and a must as thick as perfume hung in almost-visible clouds. Candles hovered above tables. Witches huddled in groups around the booths cut out from the walls, black robes bundled up around them, green faces aglow in the light.

The whispers fell like a scourge when Cresella and Walter came in, but that's how it worked with witches. A chatty bunch with nothing better to do than gossip. Cresella always imagined it was because of their line of work. When someone made potions alone all day—which itself was tedious and required time to brew—what else was there to do but gossip?

"Not exactly the yetis." She stepped off to the side near some empty tables. "Their tears." She let out a long breath. "This isn't the best first-date conversation. Walter, my business has been, well, struggling. Cookies are not a witch sort of thing, especially not enough of one to make humans line up outside the door."

"Oh," he said, placing his hands on her arms. "If you need help, I can—"

She trailed her fingers across his cheek. "You're sweeter than my cookies, but no, I don't think there's a way you can help me. Unfortunately, this little trip is the only way."

"It might be fun."

She glanced over the inn, her gaze finally falling on Helios, who was, of course, chatting up a witch. "If not for him, maybe."

"It is awkward."

"You don't say?" She grinned. "I'm going to drag him away from the women before we do end up staying the night and longer. If you need anything else, the inn sells supplies, too."

His eyes lit up. "What kind of supplies? Are they

magical? I was only able to pick up a few things quickly from home, but they weren't magical. Do we need magical?"

She picked at the thin coat he was wearing. "Coats are very magical in the way they keep the cold out and stop you from dying. Let's just worry about you having a decent one."

He glanced over his jacket and slowly nodded. "Ah, that is magic in and of itself, isn't it?"

She went around him, slipping through the inn and hoping none of the witches were paying that much attention. Of course, they were, but she could hope they would all be too busy in other gossip mills.

"Hey, Cresella!" A witch—it had to be Astrid with the way her nose was bent to the right—was sticking her head out of a booth, waving her over. Her green face glowed in tinges of red, making her all too festive.

Cresella froze, eyes gently closing and a long groan escaping. She *so* did not need this tonight. What in the devil's browned earth did that witch want?

She snuck over to her, slipping into the other side of the booth. "Astrid. I'd love to stay and chat, but—"

"You want to hear about what Helios has been up to?"

"Devil no." She crossed her arms. "Why would I want to know that?"

Astrid waved a hand around as though casting a spell. "You know, because of your…history."

"Histories are chock-full of mistakes. That doesn't mean I want to dwell on them."

Astrid nodded as a mother doting on her children. "That's good to hear. The darned satyr is all over the Hollows these days."

"Of course he is."

"Almost as bad as that human who's been around."

Cresella perked up, head turning to the side. "Human?"

"Oh, so you *haven't* heard?" Astrid grinned, wide enough it looked painful. "Let me tell you. This man's been in the Hollows a lot recently. Talking with every halfway decent-looking witch he can."

It couldn't be... Cresella licked her lips. "That's...rare. What, uhh, what does he do with these witches?"

"Talks, mostly. But he looks to get close to them. I swear Margrid said she saw him place a hand on Leigh's shoulder and lean in."

Cresella swallowed. "What's the man look like?"

"Tallish, blond hair. Decent looking, for a human that is." Astrid glanced around the room. Her hand shot over her mouth, and a finger poked toward the front desk where Walter stood. "There he is."

Before, the ground had only felt heavier, too much to tread on, when she'd seen Helios's wagon and remembered what he'd done. Now, that ground had vanished. She was falling. Chest opened up and scooped out like the insides of a newt.

Walter would never do that...would he? She'd thought the same of Helios, kept telling herself the rumors were just jealous witches going on and on. But they'd been right. What difference was there between a human and a satyr anyway? They were both horny in their own ways. And men. Men would always be men.

Walter leaned in closer to the witch at the counter and whispered something. Cresella whipped her head away and squeezed her eyes shut. Holy hell, she'd been so foolish. So dumb.

"He's a real talker from what I hear," Astrid said softly.

Cresella found her hands wound together, squeezing hard enough to turn her knuckles white. Maybe he was just talking. Just because Helios had cheated didn't mean Walter would.

Nodding, she said softly, "We'll have to watch that one."

"I just wanted to tell you because I heard he's been chatting with you. We don't wanna see another Helios incident."

"No, no one wants that. And speaking of him, you'll be happy to know I'm going to drag that satyr out of the Hollows, at least for a while." Cresella slid her way out of the booth.

Astrid perked up. "Are you two…reconnecting?"

"Strictly business. You can take my word for it." Cresella leaned over her. "I don't want to hear any rumors when I get back. Not a one."

Astrid lifted her hands. "Your secret is safe with me."

It wasn't. Though Cresella found herself caring so little. If they did get even one yeti tear, all their words and whispers wouldn't matter.

She slipped across the room to where Helios stood with his arm wrapped around a witch. He turned when Cresella stepped up, trying to slide away from the witch and failing miserably, almost stumbling over a chair and banging his horns into the wall.

"Cressy! There you are. All set?"

"Let's get this over with, Helios. I don't have the patience for this."

The other witch glanced at her, eyes narrowed, and

wrapped her hands around Helios's arm. "When will I see you again?"

Helios glanced from Cresella to the other witch. "Well, my business is… I'll be back in a day or two. Just business." He nodded as though trying to convince himself.

Cresella couldn't stop herself from rolling her eyes.

He stepped away from the witch. "Have a great evening. Let's go, Cressy."

"For once, a good idea. Let's get this over with."

"We'll have plenty of time to talk on the road." For the first time, he seemed to notice the lack of Walter. The satyr turned his head to the side. "Where is your human?"

"He's not a dog, you know." She flipped her hand around. "Off buying extra supplies, I think."

He scratched at his beard. "Yes, but you don't… Do you really think it's a good idea letting him come with?"

She wasn't sure anymore, and it hurt to admit. She led Helios to the front of the inn and stopped with the door half open, washes of cold air falling over them. "It isn't a good idea going with you in the first place, but here I am."

"If he dies along the way, it's not my fault," he muttered.

****

She was sure a hobbling, ancient newt could've been faster than Walter. When he did finally come out of the inn, he looked about, his new heavy parka almost blotting out his face. He caught sight of the wagon and Cresella and jogged over.

She, though, didn't have much to say. Astrid's words dug into her worse than a hook, and the more she struggled to free herself from them, the more they snagged and dug in. He gave a quick hello and tried to ask if anything was wrong. She feigned tiredness, got into the back of the wagon, and waited for the thing to get moving already. A trip with one cheating bastard was a pain in and of itself. But with two? Well, she might as well tie herself to a stake and hope lightning would set it on fire.

At the front of the wagon where there was a cushioned bench for the driver, Helios took his seat. He grabbed the reins, which dangled to the ground, attached to nothing, and snapped them. Two large goats, a tad bigger than horses and as thick as oxen, rose from the ground in spurts of fire. Their hooves clawed at the ground, horns ablaze in flames that would not die. With another snap of the reins, the wagon lurched forward, and they pulled away from the inn.

The road turned out of the Hollows and rolled up and away into the Razerthorn Mountains. What had once been already cold air slipped into a deep chill. Even in the winter, the Hollows had a bit of warmth, as though the snow could emanate a fire's heat. In the mountains, though, true cold reigned. Biting and deep. Burrowing through her cloak and shawl and snapping at her with the force of Cerberus's three jaws.

Near the top of the path, the peaks still far above, the harpies' homes loomed close. Sticks and leaves dangled from the ball-like nests attached to the mountain walls. Spits of smoke rose from the tops, and by each one they passed came the smoky smell of sweet cherries and apples. Harpies always loved their fruits—roasted—and nothing beat a sugared cherry roasted on a harpy pit.

As they bumped along through the mountains, the night air clear and crisp, Cresella moved farther into the wagon, trying to find a spot with more warmth and inspecting the supplies as she did. Helios had almost every ingredient imaginable, and looking at the tiny bottles, some strapped to shelves, some dangling from the roof, she picked a few out and attached them to her belt. A bit of newt entrails and black toadstool and fairy wings wouldn't put a dent in Helios's bottom line.

And after all, she was his business partner now, and a witch was no good without her ingredients. Their magic came from potions and brews, not an enchanter's words that made an item magical or a sorcerer's spells cast from their hands. Cresella rubbed her cheeks, cold and prickly from the lack of warmth. Why *did* Helios think she'd be such an asset for the yeti tears? What could she do that a sorcerer couldn't?

Of course, she used to date him. For Helios, that would be criterion enough.

Walter pulled out a small lamp from his backpack and flipped a switch. Orange glowed in the wagon and, with it, a hint of heat. She sat across from him, avoiding him as much as possible.

"Good thing I at least had the presence of mind to bring this," he said. "There's a spot over here, closer to the heater."

She looked around, almost expecting he should be talking to someone else. With a nod, she scuttled closer to him, robes rubbing against his parka.

"Are you all right?" he asked.

"Just cold," she mumbled, though her lies felt as obvious as the breath clouding in front of her; she became so suddenly sure that it was spelled out in the air, little lies drawing through her breaths and leaving a message behind.

He pulled the electric heater closer to them and held his hands out over it. "I never did thank you for letting me come."

"I admit," she said, smiling, "a human asking to take a trip through the Thicket Beyond isn't all too common. Most stay in the tourist spots. They like the pretend danger of being in the Thicket, but really, they want to be safe. They want the illusion of danger."

"No one at work will believe I did this. They would've pegged me as one of the types to keep out of the Thicket, even the safe parts."

"They saw me at the party, right? Though I'm probably not the first witch they've seen at a party of yours." Her words came out sharper than what she'd intended.

He turned his head to the side. "What? What are you talking about?"

"I talked to another witch today." She cleared her throat, and though she'd wanted to talk softer, the more she thought of her conversation with Astrid, the more a quiet fury worked through her. "Witches may tattle on about every little thing, but it's rare what they say is wrong. Which number am I? Get bored with the last green-skinned one and wanted to try something more human-like?"

"No! Never!"

"Let's make this simple. Were you talking with other witches before you came to see me?"

His head dropped. "I won't lie to you. I was talking with them, yes, but it was—"

She nodded all too seriously and pushed herself away from him. "You don't know my history, and I can't blame you for that. I thought we had time before I had to get into all the details. Apparently, that's not the case."

"You must understand I would never try to go around

on you like that."

"Walter, I…I just don't know. Do you know how many times I've heard stories like that? Even if you weren't, would this have ever worked out? Would we have ever made it? Look at us! A witch and a human. Maybe it was silly."

"I never thought so."

She worked through the wagon until she came to the flaps separating the back from the driver's bench. "I know, but right now, I just need some space to think about everything. To think about what all of *this*, if there even is a *this*, really means."

When she looked back at Walter, he was broken. She wanted to care, truly she did, but all the weight of her past had suffocated her to the point she could barely see.

She moved through the flaps and settled on the bench next to Helios. A breath of her warm air clouded in front of her, met by one of the last snowflakes drifting down from the partly cloudy skies.

"There you are," he said. "Been waiting for you."

"I had to deal with…the client. Humans can be tricky."

He gave her a wink, enough for her to cringe from. He, though, didn't seem to notice or care. "Client is it?" He put his hand on her leg. "I don't judge. I like that he's a client now. But in all honesty, it didn't seem that way in the restaurant."

She eased his hand off her leg. "Helios, I don't care what you saw or thought."

He laughed. "Ah, Cressy. You always were an odd one. In a good way. That's why I liked you. Still like you."

Realization could settle like layers of snow. At first

just a dusting, nothing more than a sheen of white over the world, but then it would come so fast, soon blanketing, covering, so deep that moving through it seemed impossible.

Was she the problem? Did she draw in someone like Walter or a cheater like Helios?

For a month, she'd debated about what to do with Helios before finally deciding to end it. She had been the laughingstock of the Hollows back then—nothing extraordinary—but this time, when the gossip of Helios sleeping around had reached its peak, the decision came easier, and somehow, someway, she had worked up the courage to end it with him. At the Wisp Tail restaurant nestled right in the middle of the Hollows, where witches would be in abundance, she'd made sure there'd be an audience.

She began to doubt herself now. She had never been courted by a warlock or even a sorcerer or wizard or lowly mage. No, she wasn't their type. No one seemed to be her type, save for Walter. Maybe her type were two-timers. She'd have to see if any fox spirits were dating.

"Helios, why did you like me to begin with?"

He smiled so sharply it could cut the snowflakes fluttering down around them. "You were different. Every man wants a taste of something exotic every now and then."

She leaned away from him. "That's what I was to you? A taste? Just different?"

He let out a long breath that clouded in front of him. "Cressy, at first, yes. I don't want to lie to you anymore. But that's what it was. I didn't think it would be anything more than a fling. But…well, I began to like you. You're not like the other witches, but in a good way. You're warmer than them. Softer."

"Those aren't *good* things for a witch." She rubbed at her forehead, feeling a headache come on.

"You don't have to be a good witch to be good." He rested the reins on his lap. "I remember a few weeks after we started dating when we were by the stream. The other witches wouldn't go close to it." He laughed. "They hated any water not in a cauldron or bathtub. But you splashed your feet in, and when I got too close to you—"

"I pulled you in the stream. Both of us." She chuckled. "I remember."

"You didn't see it, but a couple of witches passing by looked like they'd been slapped a few times. I laughed even more seeing the looks on their crinkly, old faces. That's what makes you special."

"Then why, Helios, *why* did you sleep with those other witches?"

He shrugged. "It's in the blood. Sometimes, all I see is flesh. It's not that I don't care. What can you do about it?"

Maybe it was true, but still, the answer rang with such hollowness it vibrated through her. "Helios…I gave you everything you wanted, didn't I?"

He nodded.

"Then for the love of the devil, why?"

"I can't fix the past, but if you want to try again, I can promise to never cheat again. Whenever I feel the need, I'll run straight to you and fall into your arms. Only *your* arms."

"And there it is. I figured that's what this was about." She crossed her arms. "Not in a hundred lifetimes."

"I was hoping—"

"I know what you were hoping for." She held up a

hand. "But I'm willing to settle. If possible, I'd like for us to be, I don't know, on better terms. Friends, maybe."

"Friends could work. Friends can also—"

"Just friends, Helios. *If* you aren't going to be a cheating womanizer. I don't want to be around someone like that, even as a friend." She shook her head. "Why does this have to be so hard?"

"What do you mean?"

"This," she said, waving her hands around. "Why is it so hard for me to connect with anyone, let alone find a decent person to date? You know, sometimes, I think it's my fault. I rush into things. My mother told me that whenever we were at the cauldron. *You're throwing in the ingredients too fast. Slow down. Stir slower.*" She brought her hands down on her lap, stared at the pinked tips frozen from the cold. "If I keep rushing into these things, I'll never have a stable relationship, even a friendship, before things, well, blow up."

"Is *that* what happened with your human?"

"You keep making him sound like a familiar I own."

He shrugged.

"Blow up?" She thought about it, began to even doubt Astrid and the stories, but…she'd doubted the stories of Helios back when they'd been dating. Doubted the gossip saying no one liked her, that she was the odd child out. *That* had made for awkward birthday parties sitting in the corner and watching the other children play throw the potion in the cauldron. "Yes and no. I don't know. I just need space from him."

"Cressy, I'd love to be friends. And you know what? I'm going to promise you something, my love."

"Stop calling me that."

"You see, my love, we can be friends for however

long you need. I will prove I'm a changed satyr. Then you will see. I want you to trust me. Both as your friend and new business partner and future boyfriend."

"I'm not getting back together with you."

"Time heals all wounds."

"You're a stubborn thing."

"Yes, but I have changed already. I could've been stubborn and not let the human come. But here he is."

"What a mistake that was."

He patted her leg. "I'm sure he'll get bored of this and want to go home soon. We can send him back on a passing caravan."

"That might be for the best." She sighed.

"As a friend, I'll tell you things don't always work out. That's okay. We need to look to the future, and I'm excited for us, Cressy, my love."

"As business partners and maybe, *maybe* friends."

"Yes, yes, for now. You'll see, though. Satyrs can change."

****

Not long later, they found an inn.

The Horn and Hoof barely stood out from the rocks it backed into. The top was covered in snow, a hint of the thatching underneath, and the small windows around the oval front door were frosted so thickly the light from inside was almost lost in the black of night.

Helios suggested pulling over and resting for a few hours until it would be safer to move out during the morning light. Cresella almost mentioned to him that it had been *his* idea to set out at night, that he'd said the night was a safer time to travel, with some of the more dangerous fae creatures—even the yeti they'd be looking for—asleep. Knowing Helios and his vices, he probably wanted a drink. After the night she'd been having, she couldn't argue the point.

The warmness of the inn struck like a frying pan, and the blaze of torch, candle, and firelight was the frying pan swinging back around for another smack. Cresella blinked a few times and pawed at her dark-adjusted eyes until the room swarmed into focus.

More people than she would've imagined this late at night crowded into the small dining area. Mostly mountain folk, dwarves and ice trolls and harpies, but a few centaurs clomped around, and some ghouls slunk over by the fireplace with cups of cocoa. She'd never seen an alcoholic ghoul, which made sense—dead men tell no tales, which might've been because dead men couldn't get drunk.

Helios led them to an open table near the fire, where the flames licked away the cold. Cresella rubbed her hands close to the spits of red bursting from the logs, and Walter trudged along behind without saying a word. She'd said she wanted space, and to give him credit, he'd been doing just that, keeping his distance from her and averting his eyes.

Helios patted her shoulder. "I should book the rooms. One for us, one for him, eh?"

"Do I have to go over the definition of friends again?"

"And business partners." He lifted a finger. "We'd be wasting money—" He caught her look and slowly nodded. "Three rooms, then." When he stood, he opened his arms as though ready to give a hug and grinned widely. "Hey, let's say we have a drink. They have the finest stone mud ale this side of the Razerthorns."

Walter glanced up from where he fiddled with his

fingers. "Is that made of mud?"

Helios laughed and walked off. "Silly, stupid humans. Three it is, then."

Walter played with a hangnail, wincing when a spot of blood rose. He sucked on his finger. Pulling it out, he said in a soft voice, "I…I must apologize."

"You already have." She sighed, wanting anything but to be dragged into this conversation right now. "You apologized. It's done. I just really need some space."

"I, well, yes, I understand. But I wanted to tell you, though you wouldn't believe me if I told you, so maybe it doesn't matter now." He shook his head. "Look at me, rambling on like this." He let out a long breath. "Not on purpose, but I heard the conversation in the wagon."

He'd been right there. Of course some of it would've reached him. She bit at her lip, turning her head. "It wasn't right for me to talk in front of you." She tried to force a smile. "I shouldn't have let Helios say we should send you back. It's not right. Just because you're a human doesn't mean you can't handle the Thicket Beyond."

He threw up his hands. "No, you were right. He was right." He swallowed, and a flash of pain, of regret, of something sinking in his eyes so deep they'd be lost in a pool of dark forever, arose. "I'm just a silly human caught up in things well beyond me. Even between us, well, it probably never would've worked. It was stupid, just like Luther told me."

"Luther said that?"

He flipped his hand around like it was an injured bird trying to fly. "He warned me. Said you were too different and that we could never get along. Well, I told him to bugger off." He chuckled. "Looks like he was right."

A hesitant pause, one of all that could be said, settled

between them and ate the air like a hungry deathworm. She swallowed and wondered if Luther had been wrong. What if Walter had only been talking to the other witches to ask about places they could go on dates? Or maybe he wanted to find out what witches like? She wanted to trust him. Even over a few short days, she couldn't stop thinking about his smile. Or how he checked to make sure she was okay, went out of his way to do everything right. She wanted to, but after Helios, she couldn't trust so easily. Not again.

"Maybe we should just worry about this trip for now. Yetis are some of the more dangerous creatures around."

He pushed away from the table and stood. "That's why I think it's best I go home. To give you space." He squeezed his eyes shut. "Excuse me. I need to use the restrooms. They have restrooms, I hope."

"Something of the sort." She shrugged.

And then she was alone. Flute music began to play from a troll in the corner of the room, his friends egging him on, the music growing louder and louder. It left her with a headache she couldn't shake, and she pressed her hands into her head.

How many times had she been on dates with Helios only to have the satyr disappear halfway through for "work"? He might be a jerk, but after just promising to show her that he could be different, would he really leave her?

Not that it mattered. Helios and she weren't dating, thank all the toad's wart and bog sludge in existence, but if he could break a promise this easily, what was to say he wouldn't take the yeti tear and run? He never seemed to be that kind of satyr, but she couldn't shake a feeling bubbling up in her like a potion mixed one too many stirs.

Cresella pushed up to her feet, her chair grinding into the wood, a groaning scrape roaring above the music for a moment. She walked past a group of harpies flapping above their table, voices shrill as they slapped down cards. The far side of the inn had a small bar, big enough for a handful of people to sit at. It was nothing fancy, a tree trunk rolled in and rested on two thick stumps. The smell of ale was strong—spilled puddles of it seeped into the wood, forming spots that would add to the bar's history.

An ice troll cleaned mugs with a rag. Arms, chest, and legs heavy with muscles, skin rough and thick and a greenish-blue, tusks sticking from its mouth, and long ears poking up. The bartender swiped a long strand of blue hair from his face and pressed his three-fingered hand onto the bar.

"Ma'am," he said in a voice so deep it could cause an avalanche, yet soft and more sophisticated than any troll working a backwater inn had any right to be. "What would ya like?"

"My—" Cresella sucked in a breath through her teeth. "—friend, he came by to get some ale for us, but it's been a while. I'm sure he must've gone off to the little satyr's room. I thought I'd help and bring the drinks back to our table for him."

"Satyr, you say?"

She nodded. That tone. She did *not* like that tone. Pity. Understanding.

"I saw a satyr walking past, but he didn't order any ale. I can get some for you if you'd like. We serve some of the best stone mud around."

"I've heard," she said, ice leaking into her words. "Do you happen to know what direction the satyr went in?"

He nodded toward the back where she was sure the restrooms had to be. "Back there, but I can't say for sure."

"Of course, thank you anyway." She turned and marched around the tables.

The light dimmed in the back, only a few torches bracketed into the walls. Pictures of mountains and suns rising and setting, of yetis climbing rocks, and of a group of cheering ice trolls all laughed at her as she went past— their voices like all the other witches who snickered and turned their heads.

She stopped, finding the doors for the restrooms.

Taking in a long breath, her chest rising, falling, she closed her eyes. She couldn't assume the worst with Helios. Oh, he deserved it at times, but the least he could do was show they could be business partners, and for her part, she could show a little bit of faith in his promises. Yet his words felt so hollow now. Empty. Hope and regret laced into a fool's dream.

The giggling made her turn her head. She snapped out of her thoughts and took a step toward the women's room. And there it was again. More giggling. Women were allowed to laugh and have fun putting on some makeup, but this did not sound like a couple of girls laughing about some guy at the bar they liked.

She came close to the door and pushed her ear against the wood. Fumbling. Rustling. Feet shuffling, sliding over stone. Hot breaths pumping in and out. And kisses. Kisses planted hard, then soft giggles that followed.

It didn't mean it was Helios. It could've been any couple, and what right did she have to burst in on them?

"And when I got it, rich, beyond your dreams rich," Helios said between pants. "It'll all be ours."

She let her head thump against the door. Inside, the commotion stilled before riling back up again. They didn't care, apparently. So they wouldn't mind if his so-called business partner came in.

She yanked on the door. The two stalls were at the far end of the room, but Helios and the ice troll girl hadn't gotten that far. Their clothes lay at their feet, Helios naked, pressed against her, and the ice troll with most of her clothes off. When Cresella came in, the troll shrieked and covered her breasts and shuffled for a stall, the one leg of her pants dragging behind.

He dropped to pick up his clothes, covering himself and holding up a free hand. "Cressy! I... This isn't what you think."

She took a step toward him, her hands on her hips. "Oh, this I want to hear. You were having your way with her, what, ten minutes after promising you'd show me a new side? A new Helios, right? And worse yet, I *heard* you. All for the two of you, huh?"

The ice troll yelled out from the stall, "You have a girlfriend?"

He looked to the stall and then back to Cresella and then to the stall. "No, I don't!"

"He's actually right about that one. This lovely satyr was just promising he wouldn't fool around, would try to win me back." Cresella stomped up to him and slapped him. "Cheating on me was one thing, but throwing me in the cauldron before we've even found a yeti, that's a new low. How, just how, could I ever trust you as a business partner, let alone as a friend?"

"Now, Cressy, I'd never—"

"Never lie to me? Take the yeti tear and run off?" The rage built inside her, blinding, devastating, the old pains wound into it. "If I ever, *ever* see you again, I'll drown you in a vat of bat wing stew. And I don't give a damn about yeti tears or any other business venture."

She turned and stormed out of the restroom.

The inn blurred. The music was too loud, too painful. Laughter and talk knifed in her chest. She squeezed her eyes and didn't know where to go, what to do. First Walter, now the yeti-tear venture with Helios. What did she have left?

The cold winds rushed past her, and it wasn't until the snow brushed against her cheek that she realized she was outside the inn, already far enough away that only a hint of light whispered where the inn was. She wrapped her arms around herself and stared up at the night sky. A few clouds passed by the half moon, and when they did, the night's strangle became complete. She sank into the snow and curled up and cried. Let herself cry until it seemed that was all she could do.

She didn't notice the crunch of snow until the smell reached her. Putrid and thick, of matted fur heavy with mold, only the cold to thank for locking in the worst of the smells. She slowly lifted her head and found the yellow eyes hovering in the dark. Her breath pulled in and lodged in her chest. She glanced back at the distant glow of the inn. So far. Too far.

There'd be no time. No help. By the time anyone from the inn could get to her, she'd be dead.

The yeti stepped closer, and the clouds pulled back. White light poured down from the moon.

Cresella had always heard a yeti's fur was so white that the snow would look like soot in comparison. It never made much sense. The fur being white was supposed to help them blend in.

But, oh, how it made the yeti blend in. Even with the moon and starlight, she had trouble seeing more than the yellow eyes and blackened claws. Its body was massive, thick and hulking like a boulder that had rolled in her path. The shadow it threw over her alone was a good six meters.

Its breath fogged in front of it, and for one crazed moment, she knew, somehow, she could reason with it. Holding up a hand, she said softly, "Hello, uhh, Mr. Yeti. I've heard great things about your kind. Would you…?"

When it stepped forward, it tossed back its head and let out a roar. The first swipe barely missed her head, and for once in her life, she was glad she wasn't one of the old, hobbling witches. She would've been a dead, old, hobbling witch then.

She rolled back and hopped to her feet in time to see another arm swinging. She tried to move. Screamed inside her head to move. To do anything. But her body was frozen. Maybe she knew this was it, that no witch, no human, nothing would move fast enough to stop it. In her last moments, she wanted to say she'd had a good life, but she only found a lack, a void like a bottomless cauldron that couldn't be filled, and it hurt worse than any swipe to the head would.

A man burst through the falling snow and threw a shoulder into the yeti's side. The yeti's arm whipped around in anger, going up and above her head. It turned, finding a man groaning in pain after slamming into the yeti's side and doing more damage to himself than the creature. The yeti didn't seem to know what to do with the man, whether to kill him from pity or anger.

And it was…Walter?

She could barely make out the man in the dark, but

she'd know those blond locks from anywhere. What was he *doing*?

"Cresella," he said with a moan, "run. Go!"

She had no time to explain. Truly, she had no time at all. The yeti was already reaching for Walter, picking him up like a teddy bear. What the creature would do—squeeze him till his eyes popped out, chomp out bits of his face, use him as a bat to hit Cresella—she wasn't sure.

It didn't matter. She wouldn't let it happen.

Reaching under her cloak, she frantically fumbled for something, anything. She still had the ingredients from Helios's wagon with her. If she'd been a sorceress able to cast spells, a wizard with her wand, a magi or shaman connecting with the elements—goodness, even an enchanter letting out a long spiel to cast a spell on a rock that could come to life—she'd be in better shape. But witches worked in potions and brews. All of which took a good deal of time.

Time she did not have.

Her hand settled on a bag heavy with something slimy and wet. Newt entrails. The yeti would probably think it was a snack. Her hands kept going while the yeti lifted Walter. Walter shook, the snow falling from his pants and shirt.

The yeti opened its mouth and howled. And began to squeeze.

Another bag, black toadstool. Another useless ingredient. Everything needed to be combined and cooked, no different than cookies. Her eyes felt like embers set aflame. They had to be *baked*. But they didn't have to be baked well.

In a rush, she whipped out the bag of newt entrails and a vial of black toadstool, careful to keep the two apart, one in each hand. The yeti's mouth was still wide open, fury raging from its primal screams. She'd never been great with her aim, but every once in a while, even the cursed got lucky.

She tossed the newt entrails, a slime trail dripping behind—they plopped into the yeti's mouth. Before it had a chance to react, the black toadstool whipped into its jaws right behind.

Loosening its grip, the yeti stepped back and chewed on the ingredients, mashing them together. Combining them. And the heat from inside its mouth, baking them…in a way, at least.

She cackled. "Double, double toil and trouble, what do you get when you mix newt entrails and black toadstool?" She grinned, bringing her hands together and then apart in an explosion. "Too much trouble."

Walter fell from the yeti's hands as the monster backed up, its yellow eyes small now, glimmers of fear setting in. It swallowed, burped, and grabbed at its stomach. Pops and rumbles grumbled.

Tears appeared in its eyes as bits of steam hissed from its lips. A yeti's tear. Cresella fumbled with the vial in her hand, not even realizing what she was doing until she was right under the creature. As it turned to run away, a tear whipped off its face. She raised the vial, following the drop in the moonlight, not sure it would be possible to get into the tiny glass opening. Her hands shook at the last second, a silent curse desecrating her tongue.

The tear hit the glass vial and slipped down inside where it steamed ever so slightly. She plugged up the vial and lifted it. A yeti's tear. She sank into the snow, all the adrenaline like a band of ribbons untied and let loose. Even this one tear would save her business. Do more than save it. She could open up half a dozen shops if she wanted. Maybe even a couple in the human world.

Her eyes shot wide. Walter!

She rushed to his side and knelt down next to him. "Walter! Are you all right?"

He sat up and rubbed his sides. "Tender, I suppose, but I'll survive." He tried for a smile that couldn't take off and instead settled for a weak laugh.

"What in the devil's browned earth got into you?"

He nodded back toward the inn. "I was in the little boy's room when I heard you shouting next door. I…well, I didn't mean to see it all, but I did. It seems I'm overhearing everything today." He let out a sigh. "I'm sorry. I truly am. About it all. Me listening. And…about him."

She flipped her hand around. "Don't be. I never should've trusted him. It's why we broke up in the first place, you know. He was a womanizer and liar. I hated him. Can't stand liars and—"

"Cresella, I need to say something, please."

"Walter, please, let's not do this—"

He placed his hands on her shoulders. "No, I need to. If it doesn't change a thing, then so be it. But I have to at least try. I couldn't live with myself if I didn't." He sucked in a long, painful-sounding breath. "Cresella, I told you the truth in the wagon because I do not want to lie. I have been in the Hollows the past couple of weeks. And, yes, I have been talking with other witches. But Cresella, please believe me, I've been talking to them about *you*."

"About me?"

His finger slid down to her neck where the silver locket lay. "I'd been planning this party for a while, trying to figure out a way to ask you to come. I wanted it to be perfect. So being the dolt I am, I started to ask around what you would like. Does she like pizza or curry? Fish and chips or poached egg."

"None of those things were at the party."

"They said you wouldn't like any of it."

"I did enjoy the roast beef."

He nodded. "One witch, a Matilda, I think, shrugged at the suggestion, and considering the looks I'd been getting talking about the other foods, it seemed as good a bet as any."

"So you never…?"

He shook his head. "I'm not like Helios. I'm not perfect, but I wouldn't do that."

"Walter," she said, lifting a hand and running it across his cheek, "then even this necklace…"

"I asked around what a witch would like. It was a fool's thing to do. I should've tried to figure out what you'd like on my own. But I've never been good at these sorts of things, and I wanted it to be perfect." He let out a long sigh. "I've never been a bold one, you see. Quite the opposite. Always the shy type. The odd one out. Always liking weird and odd things." He threw up his hands. "Oh, but that isn't to say that you're odd. No, I definitely do not mean that. My friends don't understand why I've been obsessing over a witch, of all things."

She smiled. "Why me?"

"I'm sure you don't remember, but a few years back, I took a trip into the Thicket Beyond. It was a graduation thing. My friends wanted to ride the brooms, and we'd have a go at it and try something crazy. But that day, I saw you. You who were so different from the other witches. So beautiful. So warm. So caring."

"First, caring and warm makes me a horrid witch, and second, how would you even know I was caring and warm?"

He smiled. "I saw you slip a cookie to a little girl waiting in line for the Make Your Own Potion exhibit."

Her eyes widened. She *had* done that. Goodness, she could barely remember it. Such a small event, so insignificant. She'd had a few extra cookies from a batch she made earlier in the day, and going by Hera's Make Your Own Potion Extravaganza, she had noticed a girl no older than five standing in the blistering heat. The poor thing had looked ready to keel over, so she'd popped a cookie into the girl's hand as she walked by. And when the girl turned to look, Cresella had pressed a finger to her lips before continuing on her way. She'd been sure no one saw her.

"I remember," she said. "But it was nothing."

"I couldn't stop thinking about it. Or you. So I came back to the Thicket Beyond when I could get a chance. It took me a while to work up the courage to ask you to the party. Far too long. So I had to make sure it was perfect because you've always been perfect to me."

She tossed her arms around him and whispered in his ear, "Thank you." A smile came, a tear of her own rolling down her cheek. "Walter, you don't think it would be too forward of me to ask for a business associate who can help set up a cookie shop in the human world? I know nothing about the place. All I know about the human world is one fantastic guy who lives there."

"On one condition," he said, leaning in closer, "a proper date first. Deal?"

She smiled. "Deal."

He kissed her, his lips lingering. Cresella understood

then what happened when ingredients met in a cauldron. And she rather liked it.

Thank you for purchasing
this publication of The Wild Rose Press, Inc.

For questions or more information
contact us at
info@thewildrosepress.com.

The Wild Rose Press, Inc.
www.thewildrosepress.com

CPSIA information can be obtained
at www.ICGtesting.com
Printed in the USA
LVHW010902160622
721261LV00013B/291